Saving Grad

Saving Grad

Karen Spafford-Fitz

James Lorimer & Company Ltd., Publishers
Toronto

James Lorimer & Company Ltd., Publishers acknowledges the support of the Ontario Arts Council (OAC), an agency of the Government of Ontario, which in 2015-16 funded 1,676 individual artists and 1,125 organizations in 209 communities across Ontario for a total of $50.5 million. We acknowledge the support of the Canada Council for the Arts, which last year invested $153 million to bring the arts to Canadians throughout the country. This project has been made possible in part by the Government of Canada and with the support of the Ontario Media Development Corporation.

Cover design: Shabnam Safari
Cover image: Shutterstock

Library and Archives Canada Cataloguing in Publication

Spafford-Fitz, Karen, 1963-, author
  Saving grad / Karen Spafford-Fitz.

(SideStreets)
Issued in print and electronic formats.
ISBN 978-1-4594-1252-1 (softcover).--ISBN 978-1-4594-1253-8 (EPUB)

    I. Title. II. Series: SideStreets

PS8637.P33S28 2017   jC813'.6   C2017-903311-5
                                          C2017-903312-3

Published by: Distributed in Canada by: Distributed in the US by:
James Lorimer &   Formac Lorimer Books   Lerner Publisher Services
Company Ltd., Publishers   5502 Atlantic Street   1251 Washington Ave. N.
117 Peter Street, Suite 304   Halifax, NS, Canada   Minneapolis, MN, USA
Toronto, ON, Canada   B3H 1G4   55401
M5V 0M3   www.lernerbooks.com
www.lorimer.ca

Manufactured by Friesens Corporation in Altona, Manitoba, Canada in July 2017.
Job #234941

*In loving memory of
Deborah Kathleen McKeown.
Forever my big sister,
forever my champion.*

Chapter 1

Curfew

Between the Thursday night sushi specials and the cold weather, we were lucky to get a table. Even so, ten of us are jammed into a booth that was meant to hold five or six people. I'm crushed against Jamal and his bulky leather jacket. On my other side, Bibi is flirting with Takeru, the cute Japanese server. Takeru's sculpted chest and shoulders are bulging beneath the tight "Naha Sushi Bar" t-shirt.

I'm taking a bite of my teriyaki roll when I glance at my phone. *9:16? Shit!*

"Gotta go!" I hope the noise in the sushi bar covers the panic in my voice.

Bibi peels her eyes away from Takeru. "But you never come out with us anymore, Vienna!" She grabs my arm. "And it's only —"

I pull away from Bibi and grab my coat and purse. I slide past Jamal as best I can. There's no way I can explain my nine o'clock curfew to them.

I reach into my purse and toss a twenty onto the table as I bolt for the door. Jamal tilts his head and looks up at me — his dark hair falling over one of his navy-black eyes. Is that disappointment on his face? I can't tell. Either way, it's time he realized I'm off-limits in the love-interest department. I start to run.

"Sorry!" I call over my shoulder to the server I nearly wipe out. Then I push through the masses of people lined up to get inside. I tug my coat on as I burst out into the biting wind. Winter hit early in Toronto this year and it hasn't let up one bit.

I race down the street to the subway stop. I book it downstairs, past the creepers hanging out inside the doors. Then I skid onto the platform. Thank god — a train is just arriving. I hop onto it without breaking stride.

Come on, come on! Hurry up! My knees bounce on the hard, curved seat.

The moment the doors open at Summerhill station, I jump onto the platform and up the stairs. My heart races as I dodge the bodies in front of me. Even when I get outside, I can't slow down. I plow straight through the puddles of slush that cover Yonge Street.

By the time I get to our house, my breath is ragged and I have a stitch in my side. I clutch it while I run up the steps. I enter the security code. But it just beeps back at me!

Oh no! My stepfather changed the code again last week! Another precious moment races by while I check my phone for the note.

"Seven-eight-four-one," I mutter as I press the keys.

I burst through the door and fling my coat into the closet. "Mom?"

Just then, he appears in the kitchen door. A scowl twists his face. Without a word, he grabs my arm and swings me toward him. His hot, boozy breath blows into my face. His grey eyes narrow and squint hard into mine. Every muscle in my body seizes up. There is white powder on his upper lip and a thin line of blood trickling from his nose. Duncan has been into more than just his single-malt Scotch tonight.

"Do you know what time it is?" My stepfather spits the words out at me. Actual spit pelts me in the face. "Did you forget about your curfew?"

His fingers are laced around my arm in a tight pinch-hold. Before I see the blow coming, Duncan smacks me in the side of my head with his other arm. My body just reacts and a scream pierces the air. *My* scream.

"I'll teach you to defy me!" he snarls.

He hits me again and I stumble to my knees. His kicks and punches start — pain firing through my body with every blow. A kick to my thigh. A backhand to the other side of my head. A push that sends me crashing into the side table. The heavy glass vase tumbles off, hitting my shoulder before it lands on the floor and shatters.

"I'm sorry, I'm sorry, I'm sorry." I'm sobbing the words over and over, trying to make Duncan stop. But he won't stop.

I push myself across the floor and skid on the broken vase. I gag when I realize the wetness dripping from my arm and chin is blood.

I'm cowering against the wall. Through my sobs, I barely hear footsteps across the hardwood floor.

"Duncan! Leave her alone! *Arrête-toi*!" Mom shoves her way between us, telling him to stop. But it's far from over.

As mad as Duncan was at me, he's even more furious with Mom.

"This is your fault!" His eyes flicker from side to side. His jaw clenches as he grabs her and shakes her. "I set up you and your trashy kid in a beautiful home. And *this* is how you repay me?"

"She was just a few minutes late." That's all Mom gets to say. Duncan's fist lands with a sickening crunch against her cheekbone.

My whole body convulses as Mom's scream pierces the air.

"She ignores my house rules!" Duncan yells. "And you let her. What else do you do while I'm hard at work?"

He emphasizes his words with blows — to Mom's head, to her stomach, to her head again and to her legs.

"Stop! Stop! *Arrête!*" Mom covers her face with her hands. As she tries to avoid the blows, Duncan kicks her legs out from under her. Mom lands hard on the wooden floor on her back.

"*No!*" I hardly recognize my own voice.

If anything, the near-silence that follows is worse than the screams. There's only the choking, shuddering sound of Mom trying to catch her breath. It leaves me gasping for air too.

I'm huddled against the wall, too afraid to move. Anything can trigger Duncan. But his energy seems spent for the moment. I force myself onto my feet. I bite my lip to stifle a sob and hobble to his decanter of Scotch. I know one thing: I need him completely blacked out.

"I'm sorry." My voice is hushed as I pick up the bottle. I pour some Scotch into a lead crystal glass. "I'm sorry," I repeat as I hand it to him.

Duncan drops onto the couch. "That's more like it." His words are slurred. "Make yourself freakin' useful for a change."

I keep pouring and Duncan keeps drinking. Before long, he's passed out.

I stumble over to Mom. "Mom," I whisper, "I'll help you to bed."

Tears and snot are streaming down Mom's face. We take one plodding step after another to her bedroom. I glance toward the other side of the bed. Living under the same roof with Duncan is enough of a nightmare. I can't imagine sleeping with that monster too.

Mom and I have lived with Duncan and his rages for two years. I know this horror story will never end. We'll never get Duncan out of our lives. He will never let us go.

But then my body jolts upright. I remember a news report I heard about a teenager who drank too much at a house party. Lying on his back, he'd drowned in his own puke.

Could it be possible?

I stagger out to the living room. Duncan is sprawled in a crooked heap on the couch. He's starting to retch and heave. But his head and shoulders are facing the floor.

Okay, roll him onto his back. Now. Do it!

I step closer. Then I take another step, and another. I'm only an arm's length away from him. But my body seizes up. I can't get any closer to him. I can't touch him.

My heart sinks as Duncan starts to puke. The horrible mess splatters onto the polished hardwood floor.

I've missed my chance.

My tears start to flow and they won't stop. All I can do is stumble to get the mop and bucket. At least that will save Mom having to clean up later.

Duncan gives one more massive heave — splashing my feet and my new jeans with puke. I wonder if I'll ever feel clean again. I wonder if I'll ever be without cuts and bruises covering my body.

Probably not.

Chapter 2

Broken Window

Duncan is a complete freak of nature. He looks fine the next day in his pressed pants and button-down shirt. The only sign he was wasted is that his fair complexion looks paler than usual. And he's going for his third shot of espresso from his fancy machine. Most people would take an Advil or two the morning after a blowout. But Duncan has heavier drugs to draw from.

"Your mother is still sleeping," he says.

"It looks like you cleaned up in the living room. Good. You can do the rest after school."

I shrink against the granite counter. Blood is seeping through both the bandage on my chin and the tea towel wrapped around my left arm. As Duncan leans in toward me, it's all I can do not to throw up.

"It looks like you could use a few stitches, sugar," he says. "You might want to visit a walk-in clinic today."

He grabs the key to his Mercedes. "And the doctor will ask," he continues. "So make sure you say that you were cleaning the window. The ladder slipped on a patch of ice and you fell." He shakes his head in fake concern. "I knew you should have waited until spring."

The smirk on his face makes me feel sick. I wish all over again that he'd died last night. But I couldn't roll him over, so he's still alive. And it's just a matter of time before he's beating on us again. There's nothing to stop him from terrorizing Mom and me.

Without another backward glance, Duncan slips out the door. He goes on his way to be Mr. Happy Pharmacist dispensing birth control pills, blood pressure meds, Viagra, and antibiotics. I wonder what the customers at his upscale drugstore would think if they knew what he was really like. Do they guess that their pharmacist beats the crap out of his wife and stepdaughter while hurling insults at them?

I make a cup of tea and take it into the master bedroom. "Mom?"

She whimpers, buried in the satin pillows on their king-size bed.

"I've brought you tea," I say. "I need to go to the walk-in clinic to get some stitches."

Mom rolls toward me. I gasp. The swelling and the bruising on her face are worse than usual.

"Looks like you need to come with me," I say gently.

"No," Mom says through swollen lips.

"And Duncan promised me it won't happen again."

"Come on, Mom. We both know —"
I look at the tears running down her swollen face. I can't say anything more.

"I'll be okay here, *chérie*." Mom moans as she passes her hand lightly across her face.

"I'll text you before I leave the clinic," I say. "In case you need anything."

* * *

The waiting room is filled with sneezing people and crying babies. I sigh. This will take forever.

I stuck another Band-Aid on my chin before I left the house. The nurse behind the check-in counter is peering at it. She's looking at the tea towel wrapped around my arm too. The concern on her face nearly does me in. I choke back the tears. I focus on her lavender-coloured scrubs as I hand her my health card. My hand shakes as I add my name to the list. I write "cut chin and arm" as the reason for my visit. Eleven people are on the list ahead of me.

I'm turning to the waiting area when the nurse calls me back.

"Vienna," she says, "we can take you in right away."

I follow Nurse Lavender down the tiled hallway to an examination room.

"Let's step in here," she says. She closes the door and removes the tea towel and Band-Aid. She looks at the gashes for a long moment. Her eyes scan the bruises on my arm. I've combed my hair over my face as much as I could, but I'm sure she can see the bump on my forehead too.

"I'd like you to tell me what happened," she says. "How did you get hurt?"

I direct my eyes down to her white lace-up shoes. She knows. And now she wants to hear it from me. I can't speak past the lump in my throat.

"Did someone do this to you?" she asks.

I dash away the tears streaming down my cheeks. Through the haze, I see Nurse Lavender waiting for an answer. She is patient, her eyes not moving from my face.

"This is the time and the place to speak up." Her voice is soft and caring. "Vienna, has someone been hurting you? It's important that you tell me."

At the kindness in her voice, hot racking sobs start deep in my belly.

"It's okay," she says. "You're safe here."

I let her words sink in as I glance around me. The room is tiny and clean. Nurse Lavender is right. I *am* safe here. But how safe would I be if Duncan found out I told on him? How safe would Mom be?

I take a deep breath. I force my eyes upward to her face. "I was cleaning the window." I sniffle. "Then the ladder slipped. I fell against the glass and it broke."

There it was, Duncan's lame excuse. I can't

believe the effort it took to repeat it. I'm beyond exhausted. I can't look at Nurse Lavender's face any longer. I feel like I've let her down somehow.

"Okay," she says, standing up. "Let me know if you would like to chat any further. You're going to need a few stitches. The doctor will be in soon."

While I wait to get stitched up, I know two things for sure. I'm too weak to make a difference. And like always, Duncan just won again.

Chapter 3

Escape

The freezing is wearing off and pain shoots through my arm and my chin. Mom and I pretend to eat the rice bowls I picked up on my way home from the clinic.

Mom has eaten a few grains of rice that she's washing down with a gin and tonic. She's been drinking more and more lately. At the sight of her bruised face, I don't have it in me to ask her about it. But the last thing this household needs is two addicts.

I'm pushing chicken and slivered carrots around in my bowl when the phone rings. My fork clatters to the floor.

"Don't answer it," Mom says.

I glance at the caller ID. "It's the pharmacy."

Mom closes her eyes and reaches for the phone. I know why she's taking the call. When Mom doesn't answer, Duncan gets crazy jealous. He accuses her of sleeping around on him. He calls her filthy names and threatens to kill her.

"Duncan?" Her brow wrinkles. I can hear that it's a female voice on the other end.

"An accident?" Mom asks. "He's in the hospital?"

I put my ear against the phone beside Mom. It's Kyla, Duncan's assistant. Mom and I know that Kyla has more than a *professional interest* in Duncan.

"— keeping him overnight for observation," Kyla says.

Mom sits here. She is in shock — from last night's beating and from the surprise phone call. The gin probably has something to do with it too.

"Sophie? *Sophie?*"

As Mom stands up, I take the phone from her hand.

"Kyla, it's Vienna," I say. I watch Mom drift into the living room. "Sorry, Mom needed to go lie down."

"Oh?" I picture Kyla twirling her blond, beach-wavy hair with her polished fingernails. "I've been trying to reach you all morning. I couldn't get through at this number or on Sophie's cell."

My teeth clench. So now we have report to Kyla too?

I scramble to think of an excuse. "Mom's just back from a yoga class," I say. "She came home early. We both have the flu. So what happened to Duncan?"

"He fell down the back stairs." Kyla chokes

back tears. "He was going out to pick up some lunch for us."

Duncan is hurt. He's not dead, but it's a start. I almost forget to act concerned. "Is he hurt badly?"

"The doctors think he has a concussion," she sobs. "He cracked his elbow and he broke his leg. They don't know yet if he might need surgery on his leg."

So finally, finally, Duncan is getting what he deserves.

"Oh no!" I remember to say. "Mom and I can't go to the hospital to see him. We've both been throwing up. Are you okay to stay there with him for a while?"

"Sure, I'm happy to." Kyla sounds like I've made her day. It's like a dream come true for her to be Duncan's loving angel at the hospital.

"Thanks, Kyla."

Even before I hang up the phone, I know what we have to do.

I hobble to the living room. Mom is lying on the couch. She's exactly where Duncan passed out last night.

"We have to go," I say. "Now."

Mom's head is bobbing. She looks like she's nodding off to sleep, and I know it's because of the gin. "What?"

"We have to grab some stuff and leave," I say. "We have to go before Duncan gets back from the hospital."

"Leave all of *this*?" Mom looks around at the leather couch and loveseat. She gestures at the baby grand piano and the modern paintings on the walls. "*C'est impossible.*"

"No, it's *not* impossible, Mom. We don't have a choice. We won't survive another night like last night."

"You aren't making any sense," Mom says. "Where will we go? How will we live?"

"I don't know. But we'll figure it out."

Mom shakes her head. Her eyes linger on her glass across the room. It's empty now. I have to get her to move before she pours her next gin and tonic.

"I know this is a nice house," I say. "But it comes with a big price tag — like having Duncan beat the crap out of us."

"But what about your grandmother?" Mom says. "Have you forgotten about *Mémère*? What if she needs us? How will she find us if we're not here?"

At the mention of Mémère, my grandmother, my eyes fill with tears. Mom and Mémère haven't been on good terms since Mom married Duncan. But I know Mom still cares about her. We're all that Mémère has left in the world.

I dash the tears from my eyes. "We'll find a way to connect with Mémère later. But we need to save ourselves first. And we need to do it now."

Mom rolls over on the couch. I leave her there crying while I stumble upstairs. I don't know how much time we have. Even if Duncan is in the hospital, Kyla will probably call again soon.

I grab my gym bag — the one I got to take to hot yoga classes. But that was before Duncan left me with so many bruises I was too ashamed to keep going. I toss in a pair of jeans, some leggings, a few shirts, socks, panties, and a pair of shoes. Then I rush between my bathroom and Mom's, collecting toothbrushes, toothpaste, soap, makeup, tampons, and Tylenol. I stuff them into the bag.

Mom is clattering around in the living room. As I step out of my bedroom, I look downstairs. She's pouring herself another gin and tonic.

"Seriously, Mom? I could use some help here!"

Mom is moving like she's a zombie. A zombie with a drinking problem and a bad limp. But she got the limp because she stepped in front of Duncan to protect me. My anger toward her fades.

I dig in Mom's closet for her leather travel bag. I stuff it full of clothes for her.

What else will we need? Identification! We'll need to show some ID to travel anywhere.

I grab Mom's passport and her birth certificate from the desk in their bedroom. I also grab the cash from the drawer.

"Where does Duncan keep his money?" I call downstairs to her.

"*Dans la chambre.*"

"Where in the bedroom?"

"In the closet," she says. "Behind his shoeshine kit."

It's not easy to find the shoeshine kit in the huge walk-in closet. I have to move the antique wooden chair to reach the ornate box stashed behind it. I want to count the money that I pull from it, but I don't have time. Whatever is here will just have to do. I'm about to put the empty box back when I notice the inscription on top.

Congratulations on your graduation, Duncan. Love Mom and Dad.

Without giving it another thought, I put the empty box under the leg of the chair. I climb onto the seat and jump down hard on it. The pain that shoots through my injured body is worth it. The leg of the chair smashes the box to bits.

"Take that, Duncan!" I leave the broken pieces on the floor.

I limp into my room to get my passport and my birth certificate. Then I remember the photos in my dresser. After Mom and Duncan got married, Duncan made us put away all our pictures of my dad, my real father. I'm not leaving without something to remember him. I pull out the picture Mom took of Dad and me a month before he died. Dad's dark hair had long-since fallen out from the chemotherapy and his skin had turned greyish-yellow. But the love on his face as he looks at me is beautiful and heartbreaking at the same time. I also grab the picture of Mom and Dad on their honeymoon in Austria. They went to Vienna, the city where Dad was born.

I'm closing the drawer when I see the arrow-patterned sash. It's the *ceinture fléchée* that Mémère made, a symbol of Mémère's Métis heritage. For years, Mémère admitted only to the French part of her background. She had faced a lot of racism growing up in western Canada. But she recently started telling others that she is not just French. She started describing herself as a proud Métis woman.

The First Nations part of her heritage was Mémère's secret for years. As I stuff the sash into my bag, I wonder how many secrets Mom and I will have to keep.

As many as it will take to prevent Duncan from finding us when he gets out of the hospital. This long history of keeping heavy secrets must run in my family.

Chapter 4

Bus Terminal

As we step out the door, I check that my
bank cards are in my purse. But if I use them,
Duncan can trace our purchases. He can find
where we are!

"Come on, Mom," I say.

We're moving at a crawl. Both of us are
hurt, and Mom doesn't want to go. But we
need to get away faster. I decide to put one
final thing on my MasterCard. I flag down a
taxi and help Mom inside.

"Downtown bus terminal," I say.

The driver's gaze lingers on my bandaged chin and Mom's bruised face. I hope the smell of cigarettes, sweat, and coffee in the cab cover up the gin on Mom's breath. We just need to get to the bus station without having to answer any questions. Without being noticed.

The driver's face lights up at the massive tip I give him when he drops us off. Minutes later, I toss the cards into a garbage can. Mom's cell phone is slipping out of the front pocket of her purse. I'm about to close the pocket when I remember — Mom and I share a cell package with Duncan. He could trace where we are that way. I drop my phone into the next garbage can. Then I reach for Mom's phone and throw it away too.

I look around, wishing our bruises and cuts weren't so visible. I really wish that Mom would stop crying. Everyone is staring at us.

"Shhh, Mom." I'm holding her up on my right side. I'm carrying both our bags on my other shoulder because I'm afraid Mom will drop hers.

I steer us around two burly security guards. They don't look like they will stop us. But having them ask if we need help would be even worse. We're nearly at the front of the line when I realize I don't know where we're going.

"How the hell am I supposed to choose?"

Mom mutters — just enough for me to know I've spoken out loud. But her muttering is no help as I scan the list: Winnipeg, Saskatoon, Calgary, Edmonton, Vancouver, Prince George. I don't know where Prince George is. But the place that is farthest away from Duncan feels like the right answer. We also need to pick somewhere we have no friends or family, because those will be the first places Duncan will look.

I've just about decided on Vancouver, but then I notice the bus for Edmonton is leaving a few hours earlier. We need to get out of Toronto as soon as we can. That decides it. As the woman ahead of us with two bouncing children walks away from the counter, I step up. "Two tickets to Edmonton, please. One way."

I dig to the bottom of my bag where I've stashed Duncan's money.

No, our *money,* I tell myself. *We've earned it in bruises and terror and nightmares.*

I hand over the cash and hoist our bags up higher on my shoulder.

"The bus will be boarding in forty minutes." The guy working behind the counter keeps looking at the tickets and money as he says this. His black curls fall over his face. I read his nametag: Azim. I like that he keeps his eyes turned down so he doesn't embarrass us any further. He's cute too. But as soon as that thought crosses my mind, I make a decision. From here on in, I'll have a strict no-dating rule. After our experience with Duncan, that's just the way it has to be.

I help Mom to the waiting area. The chatty elderly woman in the next seat offers us blueberry muffins. But I shake my head even though I know I'll be hungry later. Probably Mom will be hungry too once the gin and tonics wear off.

The forty minutes drag on. My knee is bouncing and my nerve endings are twitching. I keep scanning the bus station for familiar faces. I don't know if I'm relieved or sad that everyone is a stranger. I haven't had much of a social life for two years because of Duncan's rules and curfews. But I start thinking about how my friends and I were going to graduate together from high school this year. Now I doubt I'll graduate at all. Surviving might have to be enough.

I glance at a pay phone. I told Mémère I would drop by her place tomorrow for tea. She'll be worried about me when I don't show up. But I can't leave Mom for even one minute to make a call. And if we miss this bus, we won't have the money or the energy to try to escape again.

We finally are allowed to board the bus. I notice that the woman who offered us muffins is sitting just a few seats behind us. Still, I don't have it in me to ask if the offer still stands. Mom has fallen asleep and her head has dropped onto my shoulder. All I can do is clutch the bags that contain our few belongings as the bus rolls away from Toronto. God, we couldn't look more pathetic if we tried. Even the drunk guy who keeps switching seats to hit on female passengers doesn't pay any attention to Mom and me.

My mind circles back to how I had to convince Mom to leave at all. There we were with our fresh bruises and stitches, and she still wanted to stay because of the nice house and fancy furniture. I realize I can't drop my guard for even a minute. If we're going to build new lives and move beyond this nightmare with Duncan, I have to be the person who makes it happen. And I know something else. More than ever, Mom and I are completely on our own.

Chapter 5

Edmonton

Mom and I hardly talk for the entire two and a half days we spend on the bus. We're both blurry-eyed and cramped when we finally arrive in Edmonton. I grab our bags and step outside. The cold air makes me gasp. Mom falls hard against my sore arm as she stumbles down the bus stairs. My arm has been throbbing and I'm afraid it's getting infected. But after the money we spent on bus fare, I can't spend the rest of what we have. I need to wait before I can buy ointment to put on it.

I hunch my shoulders against the snow that swirls and blows around my face. As best I can tell, the bus depot is in the middle of nowhere. I hurry toward the building with Mom. We bypass a man with a desperate, strung-out face. He's yelling insults at two police officers. The rage in his voice reminds me of Duncan. My skin crawls. The stitches in my chin and my arm hurt even more.

Mom looks around her. "What do you think we should do next?"

"I don't know." My voice is barely a whisper. Because really, what do you do when you arrive in a strange city with no place to go and almost no money?

"There's a bus you can take to go downtown." I glance at the woman counting out coins beside us. She looks a few years older than me. I shiver and envy her the heavy winter boots and bulky, grey parka she is wearing.

"Another bus?" My words come out as a sob.

"I know," she says. "It sucks. It's just a quick ride though."

I hold my breath as we step out of the depot. Our boots crunch against the heavy snow on the sidewalks as we head in the direction the woman pointed.

"Don't they shovel the snow here?" Mom asks as we round the corner.

Even if I had an answer, the words would have been wrenched out of my mouth by the blast of wind that hits us. With my free hand, I pull the hood of my coat up over my head. But the wind slams it back down again. I wish I'd had longer to think about our destination when we were back in Toronto. I should have thought a little more before I chose Edmonton in the middle of winter. Neither one of us has warm enough clothes.

We duck our heads as we scurry into the shelter. Thank god the city bus arrives quickly.

When everyone piles off downtown, Mom and I follow.

We've hardly started walking when a hotel catches Mom's eye. "I need to lie down," she says. "We're staying here tonight."

I glance at the side of the building. I recognize the fancy gold logo and ornate lettering. How much will it cost to stay here for even one night?

"I don't think we can afford this," I tell Mom. My voice shakes.

But Mom is already inside the door. "My daughter and I need a room for tonight," she says to the woman behind the check-in desk.

The woman jumps. Her eyes grow as she takes in our cold, wet forms. I reach to adjust the Band-Aid on my chin.

"For one night," she says slowly, "that will be one-hundred and eighty-five dollars."

Mom starts to agree. Before she can say anything, I interrupt, "I'm afraid we'll have to pass."

I fix my eyes on my short leather boots. They are no match for the snow and deep cold. Mom puffs out a deep breath and I know she wants to argue with me. But I have to stay firm on this.

"Do you know of any other hotels nearby that cost less?" I ask the woman. "Like, a *lot* less?"

I look at her perfect makeup. Her pretty yellow hair is fixed into a tight, neat bun at the back of her head. I get a good look at it as she turns her head and reaches her arm out behind the counter. I'm sure she's calling security on us.

"Please," I say. "We don't want to take up any more of your time it's just that —" My throat clenches. I'm blinking hard to fight back the tears.

"It's okay." She hands me a map of downtown Edmonton. "The rates at this hotel," she says as she marks an X, "are much lower than ours. It's just a few blocks away. And," she pauses, "good luck to both of you."

Yeah, we're going to need it!

As I lead Mom away from the hotel,
I brace myself for the wintry blast. Sure
enough, it hits us the moment we step away
from the building. The wind grabs at the map
that I'm clutching in my bare hand. The snow
is coming down even harder now. The street
sign says 102A Avenue. What's that about?
I don't see it on the map at all.

"We need to go inside," I say. "I need to
double-check the map."

Up ahead, there's a big building with a
sign on the side that says "public library."
We should be able to get our bearings there.
I steer Mom in that direction.

We step inside, out of the cold and the
blowing snow. I look around and I can't
believe the number of people milling through
the main room of the library. The place is full
of parents with young children, office workers
in suits and long winter coats. There are lots
of people who — like Mom and me — look

like they just wandered indoors to escape the cold. Some of them have obviously been living on the streets for a while. I choke back a gasp. I wonder if Mom and I might end up doing that too.

"Let's rest here for a minute while I check the map again," I say.

Mom sits down in a chair by the window. I take the seat next to her. Even in this bitter cold, the sun is shining. If I hadn't just been outside freezing my ass off, the sunshine would almost convince me it's a beautiful, warm day. Too bad I know differently. I never thought I'd be so thankful for a library chair out of the cold.

Chapter 6

Jerome

I don't notice that I've fallen asleep until I hear a man's voice. My heart pounds as I clutch my bag to my chest.

"It's okay, miss." A tall man with dark eyes and hair smiles down at me. He turns to look at Mom asleep beside me, and his long, black braid flips forward onto his shoulder.

"I don't want to disturb you," he says. "But I thought you two could use some help."

I rub my hand across my face. I try to clear

the cobwebs in my brain. Beside me, Mom's bag is sitting loosely on her lap. I reach over and grab onto it.

"My name is Jerome," he says. "I work here."

He's in worn blue jeans, lace-up boots, and a plaid shirt is showing through his open parka. He doesn't look like any librarian I've ever met.

"I'm an outreach worker." When I don't answer him, he continues. "We're sometimes called social workers. We help connect people to the care and services they need to get back on their feet. It occurred to me that maybe you could use a hand."

As I'm trying to process what Jerome is saying, I wonder whether he's the next guy in line behind Duncan. Right now, I can't trust anyone at all. It seems like there will always be someone looking to take advantage of Mom and me.

"No, we're fine," I say.

Mom stirs in her sleep.

I need to get rid of this guy — Jerome, if that's even his real name. Mom might say something that will give us away.

"Okay," he says. "Just let me know if you want to chat."

I watch his broad back as he walks away from us. An oversized brown suede mitten with a beaded edge is sticking out of each side pocket. I think Jerome is First Nations. I can imagine the names Duncan would call Jerome behind his back. Not to his face, though, because Jerome is twice Duncan's size.

Jerome starts talking with a man in another chair. They're shaking hands and chatting like they're old friends. I hear that the other man is named Wayne. Wayne has torn blue jeans, a stained navy-blue ski jacket, and a bushy grey-white beard below his frayed toque. It looks like he has been living on the streets for a while.

"We'd better go look for that hotel room,"

I say to Mom.

I take the map to a woman working behind the checkout desk. "Can you tell me how long it takes to walk there?" I point to the X.

The woman pulls her reading glasses down from the top of her head. She frowns at the map. "About twenty minutes." Then she glances at my thin coat and soaking-wet boots. "Or fifteen minutes if you walk fast."

My heart sinks. Mom can't walk fast. And who am I kidding? We probably can't afford this hotel either. And if we run out of money, then it's back to Duncan.

I drop back down into the chair beside Mom. I fight back the tears. When I glance up, Jerome is looking our way. I can tell he's trying to decide if he should come talk to me again.

"Excuse me," I say to the woman behind the desk. "Do you know that man? The big guy with the braid?"

She smiles. "Yes, that's Jerome. He's worked out of the library for a few years now. He's an outreach worker."

"Thanks."

I join Mom again. When Jerome looks our way, I give him a slight wave. Then I take a deep breath and walk over to him. God, he's huge. If Duncan can inflict a horrible amount of pain, I don't want to know about this guy. But I need to take a chance. Just one careful chance.

"Um, Jerome? Maybe we could use some help after all," I say. "Mom and I — we don't exactly have a place to stay tonight. Even the cheap hotels cost too much money. So if you have any ideas . . ."

"I have a few ideas." Jerome's eyes linger on my chin. "You might be looking for a women's shelter. To get away from an abusive situation."

He pauses. I keep my face pointed straight ahead. I don't agree or disagree with him.

"If that's so," he says, "I could take you and your mom to the social services office."

I still don't say anything.

"They'd have some questions for you. Like whether you have any money to get through the next few days. And they'd need to verify who you are and your situation."

My heart hammers. I imagine that information trickling back to Duncan.

"We're not answering any questions," I say.

"Can you at least tell me if you have some money?" he asks.

Every muscle in my body tenses. How do I know he isn't going to steal the little money we have left? My arm and shoulder are sore from the tight grip I have on my bag.

"Because if you have some money on hand," Jerome says, "I know of websites you could check out. There are some people around the city who let out apartments for short-term rentals — sometimes even on a day-by-day basis. They're cheaper than hotels.

You often have the option of staying on longer if you wish."

I still don't say anything, but Jerome seems to have made up his mind.

"Come on." Jerome stands up. "I'll log on to the computer for you. Then you can check them out for yourself."

I've set the search parameters on the rental site to show the cheapest places first. One ad has big letters across the top that read "NO BEDBUGS OR COCKROACHES!" It makes me shudder.

Mom grimaces in pain as she lowers herself into the chair beside me. I don't look at her face. I'm afraid these tiny, run-down places will have her scurrying back to Duncan. And where would that leave me?

I scroll through place after place. We can't afford to stay in even the cheapest places for more than a few weeks. And who knows how long it will take us to find jobs and get our first paycheques?

"Any leads?" Jerome pulls up a chair alongside us.

"Nothing." I choke back a sob. "Even the cheapest places cost too much. Some of them want first and last month's rent. And damage deposits too."

Without saying a word, Jerome hands me a slip of paper.

"Yulia Zelinski?" I read. "Who's she?"

"Yulia is someone I know. She's rented her basement apartment to a few other people I've met here. The place isn't big and it isn't fancy. But it's clean and Yulia is a decent woman with a kind heart. I just phoned her. Her last tenants moved out two weeks ago. She said you can go meet her tonight if you want."

Beside me, Mom starts thanking Jerome. Maybe I should do the same thing. But what if he's leading us into a trap?

"Does this Yulia woman live nearby?" I ask.

"Not exactly," Jerome says. "She lives in the west end. It's near a bus line though. Would you like to go check it out?"

"Oh, yes," Mom says.

I scowl at Mom. How could she instantly turn into Jerome's best friend? But we do need a place to stay.

"Here, I'll draw you a map on the back." Jerome takes the paper and pulls out a pen. "The bus goes straight across Stony Plain Road." When he sees my blank expression, he adds, "I'll walk you to the bus stop. It's not far. So you take the bus until you get here." He scribbles down a street number. "Then walk two blocks north. Turn left. Yulia's house is third on the right."

Jerome pulls out his cell phone. I look at it longingly as he makes the phone call.

"Yulia," he says. "It's Jerome again. I'm just taking, um —" he looks at us. "What are your names?"

My stomach quivers. But Mom answers

right away, so I quietly say my name too.

"I'm just taking Sophie and Vienna to the bus stop. They'll be at your place within the hour." He pauses. "Thanks, Yulia. We'll be in touch."

We'll be in touch? What the hell does he mean by that?

Jerome zips up his coat and pulls on his heavy mitts. The cold bites at my toes and my face as we walk through the open square — Churchill Square it's called. Mom limps alongside me.

As we say goodbye to Jerome, I wonder again if it's a trap. My heart sinks. What if I don't have the strength or the courage to get us out of it?

I take a deep breath. Then I step onto the bus.

Chapter 7

"Cheap Like Borscht"

We step out of the bus onto the icy sidewalk. A man hovering around the bus stop leers at me. Mom and I hurry past him.

We turn the corner and I look for house numbers in the darkness. Yulia's house is the one with the blue paint peeling off it. I don't trust the handrail that tilts outward beyond the concrete steps. Mom and I grab it though as we step around the icy patches leading up to the front door.

An elderly woman opens it almost before I take my hand away.

"Hi," I say. "Are you Yulia?"

She gives a tight little nod. "Your names?"

"Vienna and Sophie."

She still doesn't say anything. But she looks us over.

"Jerome sent us," I add.

"You come in now." She steps aside. "Jerome — he's a good boy."

I hope Yulia is right about that.

As we step inside, a smell hits me square in the face. It's something like dirt, and maybe mould or rot. It's not like anything I've ever smelled or eaten before. And I sure wouldn't want to eat it, even though I'm starving. Meanwhile, the flickering light in the front landing and the swirly patterns in the faded brown wallpaper are adding to the pukey feeling in my stomach.

Yulia's eyes flit over my stitched chin and Mom's swollen lip. "You leave your boots here."

As she speaks, Yulia touches the dark grey kerchief that covers most of her hair.

It takes me a moment to understand Yulia's accent. But then I pull off my soggy boots. My socks are soaking wet underneath.

"This way," she says. "Downstairs."

My heart hammers as we follow her. Yulia turns on another light at the foot of the stairs. I catch my first glimpse of her apartment. The faded chicken-gravy coloured carpet with the dark stains. The lumpy, mismatched couch and armchair. The metal table and chairs in the far corner beside the stained fridge and stove.

Yulia is waiting for us to say something. But Mom and I are both speechless. Yulia sighs and pushes open a door. "And in here," she says.

I brush past her to check out the bedroom and the bathroom. Both rooms are cramped and musty. I really want to leave. But I don't have the strength to head back outside again.

"Six-hundred dollars for one month," Yulia says.

Six-hundred dollars? That would leave us with nothing!

Yulia's eyes widen when she sees my face. "Six-hundred dollars," she says, "is cheap like borscht."

"Cheap like *what*?"

"Borscht. Beet soup," she says. "What is cooking upstairs."

Then I remember what Jerome said about short-term rentals. "Could we pay you for one week only? Mom and I are just getting settled and . . ."

I glance over at Mom. She has perched on the edge of the wildly patterned couch as she stares around the room.

"I could pay you right now," I say. "In cash."

Yulia nods. "Fine. One week," she says. "One-hundred fifty dollars today. Then one-hundred fifty dollars next week. In cash."

Keeping my back turned toward Yulia,

I reach into the bottom of my bag and pull out some bills. I count them carefully and hand them over.

"So one week," she says. "And no parties here. And no drugs and no alcohol."

Drugs and alcohol? Those are Duncan's favourite things.

"That won't be a problem," I say.

Yulia nods. "Good," she says. "You have more things to move in?"

"No," I say. "This is everything we have."

Yulia nods and then leaves us in our new home.

For the rest of the week, Mom and I hole up in the apartment. My stitches are itching like crazy. I hope that means they're healing. The doctor at the clinic in Toronto told me to come back after a week to get them out. That's not going to happen, so I've been preparing Mom to remove them for me. I found a little pair of cuticle scissors in the bottom of my makeup bag, so at least we won't have to buy a pair.

So far, we've bought a few groceries and some shampoo. But today I pull a package of hair dye out of the plastic grocery bag.

"Does 'medium auburn red' sound good, Mom?"

She scrunches her nose up. "Not for me. I'm holding on to the nice hair colour Marnie gave me as long as I can."

I can hardly blame her. Mom's expensive highlights and dyed hair probably cost about three weeks of rent to Yulia.

As I step into the bathroom, I call back to Mom. "We have spaghetti sauce for dinner. But we're out of pasta. Can you go get some?"

While I comb the dye through my hair, Mom trudges up the stairs to the back door. She hasn't been out of the apartment on her own since we got here. We've been jammed into this tiny apartment — even sharing the double bed. I feel like I can almost breathe again now that I'm alone.

I rinse the last of the hair dye down the sink. A long, hot bath would feel amazing. But the apartment only has a rusty old shower stall, so I'll take a longer-than-usual shower instead. I'm just stepping into it when I hear Mom coming back downstairs.

When I finally emerge from the bathroom with my newly-red hair, Mom is pouring herself a gin and tonic at the table. Given the level in the gin bottle, it isn't her first drink.

"Are you kidding me?" I shriek. "We don't have enough money for booze!"

Mom waves her free hand. "I just felt like a drink," she says. "*C'est tout.*"

"Yulia said no alcohol." I lower my voice. "Are you trying to get us thrown out of here?"

Mom collapses into a chair, her hand covering her face. "Right now, I don't know what I'm trying to do. Other than figure out if we were too rash in leaving Toronto. Maybe

Duncan has learned his lesson. Maybe he won't do it again."

The rage nearly chokes me. "Did you really just say that, Mom? The only thing Duncan has learned since we left is how to shove more pills down his throat. Do you think he's healing quietly without them?"

I'm shaking as I move toward Mom. "I'll tell you this for sure. If we go back, we'll never come out of that house alive. So you can go back to that monster if you want." I'm about two inches from her face now. "But you will never see me again."

Chapter 8

Unstitched

After the blowout with Mom last night,
I couldn't fall asleep. But now I've slept in.

"Mom? *Mom?*" I call.

She's not here! What if she's calling Duncan right now?

I pull on some clothes. I'm dashing up the stairs when I nearly run into Mom.

"Come back downstairs with me," she says, leading me back into the apartment. "I have some news for you."

I'm not sure if I'm ready for this.

"I got a job," Mom says.

"A job?"

"Yes, a job. And don't look so surprised. I thought about what you said last night. You were right. We can't go back to Duncan. So I got a job."

"Where?"

"At Starbucks. When I was coming home yesterday from the liquor store . . ." Her face flushes. "I saw a sign that said Starbucks was hiring. So I went back today to fill out an application."

"And they hired you?"

"Of course," Mom says. "Think about all the fancy coffees I made for Duncan on his espresso machine. The manager at Starbucks was totally impressed."

I feel rooted to the spot. This is good news. But how much information did Mom have to give about us to get this job? At least Smith, the last name Mom took when she married

Duncan Smith, is common. It would be hard to track a Smith, even with a first name like Sophie. But what else did Mom tell them at Starbucks?

"Did they ask you for references?"

"Yes," Mom says. "I told them I've been home raising my daughter for the last decade so I don't have any. They were fine with that, especially when I said I can work whatever hours they need me to." Mom smiles. "I start Friday afternoon."

"Two days," I say. "So once I find a job too, we'll be all set."

"Actually, Vienna, I need to talk to you about that. You getting a job, that's not going to happen — unless it is absolutely necessary," Mom says. "You told me your terms last night — about what you'd do if I go back to Duncan. And now I have some terms for you. School has to be your top priority. I need to see that high school diploma in your hand at the end of this school year."

Wow. School completely fell off of my radar screen once we left Toronto. But I can see Mom's point about the diploma. It's one more step toward freedom from men like Duncan.

Then I remember something else. "Sure thing, Mom. I'll register at a new school," I say. "But first I'll need you to remove the stitches from my chin."

"*Merde!*" Mom says.

"You can say 'shit' all you want. But there's no way I'm starting at a new school looking like Frankenstein," I say. "So let's do this."

You'd think that living with Duncan for more than two years would make Mom a pro at dealing with stitches. But even with me helping her, it's taking forever. My chin is growing sorer with every awkward try she makes to tug out another stitch.

"Ouch!" I cry. "Mom, just put the scissors under the knot and cut the thread."

"*Oui*," she says. "I know. But I can't hold my hand steady."

At least all six stitches are out of my arm now. With only three stitches left in my chin, it feels like time for a break. Mom limps into the kitchen and pours herself a gin and tonic. She gives me a sideways look like she's waiting for me to give her a hard time about it. But since I have something else on my mind, I decide not to say anything about her drink. I watch her swallow it in big gulps.

"I've been thinking, Mom," I say. "What if Duncan is trying to find us? It's better if we don't use our real names when I register at my new school."

"That won't be so easy," Mom says. "When you changed schools two years ago, I had to show ID for both you and me. There's no way a school will accept a name that's different from what it says on your birth certificate."

"Oh no!" My pulse races. I feel like pitching a major fit right here on the spot. "But it might make the difference between Duncan finding us or not."

I step into the bathroom to splash cold water on my face. I try to avoid touching the three stitches still poking out from my chin. When I step back into the living room, the drink level in Mom's glass is higher than it was. I can't have her drinking at all. What if she gets careless and says something at work? Or loses her job? I make a mental note to watch her more closely in the days ahead.

"You're probably right," I say. "I'll have no choice but to show my ID when I register. But if we can possibly work around having to use my real name, I want to stop going by Vienna Bauer. And I know which last name I'd like to use."

Mom turns and looks at me.

"Fleury." I try to calm my breathing while I wait for her response. "We could become Sophie and Vienna Fleury."

"Fleury," Mom says. "Mémère's last name."

"I think it's beautiful."

"It *is* beautiful." Mom twirls her glass in her hand. She doesn't say anything. I can tell she's thinking about the fight she had with Mémère before marrying Duncan. Dad had just died and Mémère thought Mom was moving too fast into another marriage. I agreed with Mémère. And Mom hasn't spoken to Mémère since. I think it's because Mémère was actually right.

"Maybe you could phone Mémère and —"

"*Non*." Mom gestures around the room. "Not while I'm living like *this*."

"This is hardly a time to be proud, Mom," I say. "And living here sure beats having Duncan attacking us. Maybe even killing us next time."

She swallows the rest of her drink.

"I *am* going to tell them I'm Vienna Fleury at my new school. It's worth a try," I say. "And you remember we still have three more stitches to take out, right?"

"*Mon Dieu*!" she says. *My god!*

I hand her the cuticle scissors again. I clench my teeth and hope the last three stitches come out more easily than the others have.

Chapter 9

Vienna Fleury

Yulia tells me the nearest high school is Ashton Heights. She looks about eighty-five. I suspect that her information isn't totally up-to-date. But I don't have a computer or a phone to check for myself. I'll have to take Yulia's word for it.

I'm not eighteen until August, so Mom has to come with me to register. She seems extra nervous about it. Even though the clock on the stove says it's almost noon, Mom is still rattling around in the bedroom getting ready.

I'm pacing around the living room when I remember something else I need to do. I grab my purse and I dump it upside-down onto the kitchen table. I can't remember when I last cleaned it out. Now I need to get rid of everything that could connect me to my old life with Duncan.

I put the chapstick, the lipstick, the tampons, and the eyeliner back into the purse. They're completely harmless. So are the breath mints, the Kleenex, the pen, and the little bottle of Motrin. But when I look at everything else, my stomach clenches into a knot.

All the receipts — from Aritzia, Victoria's Secret, Aldo, and Shopper's Drug Mart — have Toronto addresses on them. I stuff them into a plastic bag to recycle later, along with the stamp card from the salon where I used to get my eyebrows waxed. I pick up the instructions the doctor at the clinic gave me: "Caring For

Your Stitches." I wonder what she'd say if she learned that I *cared for my stitches* by bullying my semi-drunk mother into removing them with tweezers and cuticle scissors. I stuff the printout into the plastic bag too.

My birth certificate and my passport worry me the most. They're dead giveaways. I'd like to shred them to pieces, but I need them to register at school — or if Duncan turns up and we have to bolt again. Duncan's huge, twisted ego will never stand for Mom and me taking off on him. It's not that he loves us, but he's convinced we belong to him. And he needs us there to verbally and physically abuse. He needs to prove what a big, powerful man he is.

I'm putting my ID back in my purse when a paper sticking out of the back pocket catches my eye. It's where Jerome wrote out Yulia's phone number and the directions to our apartment. I'm still finding my way around Edmonton so I leave it in my purse. I might get turned around while I'm on the transit system. Since this is from my *new* life, it's not a problem anyway.

"Are you ready to go yet?" I call to Mom.

"I guess so." Mom is running her hands through her hair. She is buttoning and unbuttoning her grey cardigan. She looks like she would rather just stay here with a good stiff gin and tonic, although I'm sure not going to suggest that.

"Let's go then," I say.

I brace myself as we step outside the apartment. It's a little warmer than when we first arrived, but that's not saying much. Even for the short walk to the bus stop, the wind bites through my jeans. I clench my toes in my boots as we veer around patches of ice on the sidewalk. It's a relief when we get seats on the bus.

Just when I'm sure we've missed our stop, a red brick building appears. Sure enough, it's Ashton Heights High School — just like Yulia said.

A tall man is briefing a secretary when we step inside the main office. They stop talking and look at us. The man squints at us from behind his little round glasses.

"I'd like to register for grade twelve," I say.

"Wonderful." A smile lights up his face. "Welcome to Ashton Heights. I'm Mr. Shah, the principal. I hope you'll be very happy here."

Very happy seems like too much to expect. If I can leave with a diploma in my hand at the end of the year, that will be amazing.

"I'm dashing away to a meeting," he says. "But Jasmine will help you." He nods toward the woman with orange glasses and masses of grey-brown curls.

Jasmine smiles up at us. "Okay," she says. "Let's start with your identification. Did you bring that with you?"

My hand shakes as I pass her my birth certificate.

"So you're Vienna Bauer?" she asks.

"Sort of." I take a deep breath. "Actually,

my last name is going to change. Because we're going through a divorce. We're both going to be using Mom's maiden name."

Mom tenses beside me. Before she can say anything, I rush on. "So I'd like to go by Vienna Fleury."

The frown on Jasmine's face makes my stomach tighten. "Unfortunately, I have no choice," Jasmine says. "I have to put your name — as it appears on your birth certificate — into the official register."

My shoulders slump forward.

"Once your name change has been finalized," she says, "bring the papers to me and we'll switch everything over.

"But in the meantime," Jasmine continues, "I can ensure that your name appears on the teachers' class lists as Vienna Fleury. How does that sound?"

I know this is the best I can hope for. Nobody at Ashton Heights will know me as anything other than Vienna Fleury. It's enough.

"Good. Thank you," I say.

Jasmine smiles and hands me a brochure. "These are the grade twelve courses we offer. The new term started three weeks ago. Some of the classes are pretty full, but let's see what we can do."

I look them over. "I did Math, Chem, and History last term," I say. "I still need English to graduate. And I started French and Business back east before Mom and I moved here."

Jasmine pulls up class lists on her computer. "I can definitely put you into English and French," she says. "The Business class is pretty full. Mr. Demko might grumble a bit, but I think we can make that work too." She keys in my name. "And are you starting classes today?"

I nod.

"Lunch period is almost over," she says, "so you've missed Business. But you can still catch English and French this afternoon."

I was so nervous about registering for school that I came empty-handed. The pen in the bottom of my purse is all I have to work with. Jasmine smiles and hands me a pad of paper from her desk.

"Here you go," she says. "If that's not enough paper to get you through the afternoon, come back and see me."

Her eyes crinkle in a friendly way behind her orange glasses. Even though I know better than to let my guard down, I decide I like her.

Jasmine turns to Mom. "It's nice to meet you too, Sophie," she says. "Welcome to Edmonton."

Chapter 10

Ashton Heights High School

The bell goes. Suddenly bodies are streaming down the hall on both sides of me. After poring over the school map Jasmine gave me, I think I've figured out where my English class is. On the way, I stop at the bathroom to dot some concealer on my chin. I curse Duncan all over again for hurting me in such a visible spot. At least the injury on my arm is easier to hide. After one last glance in the mirror, I take off to class.

The teacher isn't there yet but most of the chairs are taken. I slip into the empty chair nearest the door. A tall girl in tight yoga clothes bursts into the room. She stands in front of me. "That's my seat, redhead," she sneers at me. "Move your ass."

Laughter breaks out around us. Trust me to meet the class bully on my first day. Without a word, I slink off to another seat at the far back corner.

Ms. Sandor is barely through the door when she starts talking about *Hamlet*. It's the Shakespeare play we'll be studying this term. She doesn't pause for a breath as she tells us about Hamlet's troubled relationship with Claudius, his stepfather. She explains that Hamlet feels his mother married Claudius too quickly after his father died. Hamlet gets obsessed with wanting to kill his stepfather. Man, can I ever relate to that.

I sit up straighter in my chair to listen. Then I wish I hadn't, because that's when the teacher notices me. "I'm sorry," Ms. Sandor says. "You are . . . ?"

"Vienna Fleury." I try to speak loudly enough for her to hear me. It feels good saying "Fleury" for my last name. That is, until Ms. Sandor makes me repeat it a dozen times to make sure she has it right in her book.

I keep my head down for the rest of the class. I'm dreading French class next period, where everyone will check me out all over again. All this attention is wearing me down.

Madame Montclair's classroom is way at the other end of the school. She's talking to some students at the front of the room when I enter. I keep my head down as I slide past them. I drop into an empty seat near the notice board. The sign in the middle says, "Hope For Haiti: Can You Help?" Posters of flooded streets and people living in makeshift tents cover the rest of the space. It seems natural disasters — tropical storms, floods, hurricanes, and earthquakes — have hit Haiti, one right after the other.

I look back to where Madame Montclair is having a lively conversation. Her hands are waving across her brightly patterned dress. She brushes back the tight, black braids that have escaped her striped hairband.

Every one of my nerve endings feels frayed. It's like I'm on the brink of unravelling right here. I need to get this class over with so I can get the hell home.

There's a short girl with a big smile sitting a few chairs over from me. She's trying to catch my eye, but I'm doing my best to ignore her. I think she was also in my English class. I remember my "no dating" policy and decide something else: I'd better avoid making any friends at all — both male and female.

I force myself to stop touching my chin so I don't rub off the concealer. I realize then that Madame Montclair is asking me my name.

"*Je m'appelle Vienna Fleury,*" I answer.

Madame Montclair asks me some more questions. I vaguely notice that the other students are watching us, their eyes wide. It's only then that I realize Madame Montclair and I have been speaking French.

"Wow," someone behind me says. "She's really good!"

Oh no! I didn't mean to draw any attention to myself.

But Madame Montclair is smiling at me. Her dark-brown eyes sparkle as she welcomes me to Ashton Heights.

I mutter a quick "*merci.*" Then I focus on the posters pinned to the notice board again. I try to block out everything, especially the same girl who was trying to get my attention before class. Her name is Mandy and she raises her hand every time Madame Montclair asks a question. The way she mangles the French language hurts my ears and chops away at my frayed nerves even more.

I heave a sigh of relief when the class is finally over. My stomach is growling. The effort it took to get through my first day was exhausting.

I'm almost at the main doors when Mandy falls into step beside me.

"Hey, new kid," she says. "I'm Mandy Mok. And you're Vienna?"

I nod.

"Well, just so you know, Caprice always greets new students with 'move your ass.'"

"What?" Then I remember the girl in English class. My face flushes with heat.

"Oops, I wasn't going to mention that." Mandy frowns. "It's gotta suck moving partway through your last year of high school."

Girl, you have no idea! I think.

"So where did you move from?"

Uh-oh! I've had so much on my mind that I didn't work out a backstory. "From out east," I mutter.

"Cool," Mandy smiles. "Whereabouts?"

Beads of sweat are dripping down my back. "Um, Montreal."

"So *that's* why you're so good at French."

"Yeah," I say. So right on the spot, I become a Francophone girl from Montreal.

"Well, you're lucky," Mandy says.

Lucky? What?

"I suck at French. My parents expect me to get nineties in all of my classes," she says. "As if *that's* going to happen. And they want me to stop signing up for stuff until I've raised all my marks. It's hard though. I'm what you'd call a 'joiner.'"

"A joiner?" My brain flat-out hurts now.

"You know, someone who joins a bunch of clubs and committees. It drives my parents nuts."

God, will she ever stop talking?

"Speaking of which," Mandy says, "some Grade Twelve students are starting to plan the grad party. We're looking for more people to join the committee. You interested? It'd be a great way to meet a bunch of people at your new school."

A bunch of people? That's exactly what I need to avoid!

"There'll be an assembly next week to learn more about the grad party committee. Maybe think about it, okay?"

I don't stick around to give Mandy an answer. It's all I can do not to break down in tears. The scars on my chin and my arm are itching like crazy. I need to get out of here. I think I tell Mandy "goodbye" before I dash across the street to the bus stop. But I can't say for sure.

Chapter 11

News From Mémère

I spend the next week catching up at school. French is really easy. All I have to do is focus on Mr. Demko's supply and demand charts in Business, and Ms. Sandor's lectures about *Hamlet* in English. Meanwhile, trying to find ways to live even more cheaply is grinding me down. I nearly cry when I have to hand Yulia the next hundred and fifty dollars for rent. It feels like forever before Mom gets her first paycheque. At least Mom is working closing shifts at Starbucks. She gets to bring home the baked goods and yogurt parfaits that are about to expire, so that helps.

Still, my days and nights are filled with wondering if Duncan is trying to find us. I've stopped worrying about Jerome coming for us here. If that were his plan, he would have shown up already. Thank god I decided to trust him.

Our apartment is far from perfect. The walls and the ceiling are so thin that we hear Yulia snoring every night. When she flushes her toilet, the basement shakes like a freight train is running through it. But our cramped, "cheap as borscht" apartment is starting to feel like ours. We've set out the photos I brought from home. I draped Mémère's *ceinture fléchée* across nails on the living room wall. The colourful sash matches Yulia's gaudy furniture as well as anything could.

I finish writing a response to a passage in *Hamlet* and decide to call Mémère. I'd held off until we were settled so I could tell her we were doing okay. I'm surprised to realize that we actually *are* doing okay.

There is a pay phone a few blocks away. I stomp my feet to thaw them when I'm inside the phone booth. As I dial Mémère's number, I try not to think about how the receiver reeks of beer and cigarettes and onions. It also smells like someone took a piss in here.

"*Allô?*"

I nearly sob when I hear that sweet voice. "Mémère," I say, "it's me. *C'est moi.*"

"Vienna, *chérie! Que tu me manques!*"

"I miss you too, Mémère. How are you?"

"*Ça va,*" she says. "*Et toi et Sophie?*"

"We're okay too." I choke back the lump in my throat. "I'm sorry we left without telling you. But we had to. Duncan was —"

"He was hurting you?" Mémère says.

"*Oui.* Yes. We had to leave fast."

"*Mon Dieu.*" She sounds worried, but not too surprised. "Where are you now?"

90

I pause. "It's better if I don't tell you, Mémère. Duncan might ask you about us."

Mémère doesn't say anything for a moment.

"He's already come to see you, *n'est-ce pas?*" I say.

"*Oui.* And his leg," she says, "it was *blessé.*"

"It was hurt? In a cast?"

"*Oui,*" she says. "Duncan said he and Sophie fought. And then she left with you. He said that if I was talking to you, I should say he wants you to come back —"

"That's not going to happen," I say.

"*— et qu'il vous aime.*"

And that he loves us. A gag catches in my throat at the thought.

The whole time we've been talking, I've been dropping coins into the pay phone.

"Mémère, *je dois partir.*" I tell her I have to go. "And please don't worry about us."

Mémère is sobbing. Tears fill my eyes and the street lamp outside the phone booth blurs.

"*Et je t'aime*," I say. *I love you.*

At that moment, the phone cuts out.
I don't know if Mémère even heard me. I put
the receiver back in place and step out into
the cold.

✱ ✱ ✱

The next morning, Mandy looks at my coat
and frowns. "Why are you wearing that
inside?"

"I haven't found my lock yet," I lie.
"It's still buried inside one of the boxes from
our move."

I bought binders and lined paper at the
dollar store last week, but I cheaped out about
buying a lock.

"You can put your stuff in my locker,"
Mandy says.

Since we left Toronto, I've been taking my
few belongings everywhere I go. At this rate,
I'm turning into a hoarder as well as a liar.

"No thanks," I say. "I might need it."

"No you won't," Mandy says. "The grade twelve assembly is this afternoon. It's always hot and sweaty in the gym. Just hang your coat in here."

Mandy tells me her combination. She is closing her locker when shouts break out down the hall.

"Don't ignore me, you slut!" It's Caprice. She appears behind Fatima, a girl from my Business class.

Slut? Really? I've never heard Fatima even answer a question in class, much less talk to a guy. She wears dark, loose clothing and her long hair covers much of her shy, brown face. Fatima seems to want to make herself invisible. I can sure relate to that.

"I saw you leave his place last night," Caprice yells.

"I just dropped off some Chem notes."

"Chem notes, my ass!" Caprice shoves Fatima, whose head cracks into the locker.

"It's true." Fatima's eyes are darting from side to side. "I swear it is."

Kids start swarming around them. A sour, sick feeling spreads through my body. I want to help Fatima but I can't move. Fatima's stricken face and cries send my thoughts crashing back into the years of Duncan's abuse. My arm and chin burn as though the injuries are ripped wide open. And like a sick horror movie, the many terrified nights play out in my head.

I try to choke back my panic. But I can't swallow and I can't breathe. My heart is pounding and the blood is rushing in my ears. I'm so hemmed in by bodies I can't move. I drop to my knees and cover my eyes — then my ears — with my hands. I try to block everything out.

"Vienna? *Vienna* — what is it?"

Mandy is crouched on the floor beside me.

When I can focus again, the fight has ended. Caprice is mouthing off to Mr. Shah as he takes her to the office. Mrs. Singh, a Math teacher, is leading Fatima away. Fatima is sobbing.

Mandy turns to talk to the kids around us. "It's okay," she says. "Vienna just felt sick. I think she's getting the flu."

When the crowd has left, she turns back to me. "Vienna, my god! What was *that* about?"

"It's like you said." I take a breath. "I thought I was going to throw up. Plus, uh, cramps."

Someone speaks up behind me. "Vienna, do you need some fresh air?"

"Actually, we do," Mandy says. "If it's okay, I'd like to stay with her."

Mr. Demko adjusts his wire-rimmed glasses. "I'll mark you both down as excused absences. Are you sure you're all right, Vienna?" The concern on his face nearly makes me cry.

"I just need some fresh air," I choke out.

I bolt out the double doors. Once I'm outside, I take long, deep breaths.

A few minutes later, Mandy pushes the door open. She is clutching her hoodie around her. "God, Vienna. It's freezing," she says. She swipes her black hair off her face as I step back inside. "That was pure terror on your face. What was going on back there?"

"Wouldn't you be scared of puking on Caprice?"

"Yeah, I guess. But —"

I can't let her press me further. "So the grade twelve assembly," I say, "it's about the grad party?"

Mandy nods and smiles. "It's right after lunch. And seriously, you need to sign up for the grad party committee. You know — to finish high school on a positive note."

I picture students snapping selfies and posting photos all over social media. I shouldn't even go to the grad party, much less organize it.

"I don't think so," I say.

Mandy's face grows serious. "I haven't

known you for long," she says. "But it seems like you don't have much fun."

If you only knew! I think.

"So this is your chance," she says.

I sigh. Mandy is right about one thing. I have no idea how to be fun. I had it beaten out of me a long time ago.

Chapter 12

Safe Grad

Mandy had to be in the gym early, so I make my way to the assembly by myself. I pass the main office and see Caprice sitting with her arms crossed and a scowl on her face. Jasmine looks up and smiles at me, then she returns to her typing.

Jasmine has started dropping by Mom's coffee shop after school. Mom says it's nice to have someone to talk to. Without Duncan around, Mom can actually make some friends. She has the regulars from the coffee shop and the people she meets when she's waiting for the bus. Mom is doing better in the friend department than I am. I just hope she hasn't told Jasmine too much about us. All we need is for someone to put together why Mom and I had to leave Toronto. What if Duncan started looking for us and that got back to him?

I step inside the gym. Mandy waves at me from the front where she sits with the rest of the committee.

"Welcome to all of the Grade Twelve students and teachers," Mr. Shah says as he takes the mic. "In a few minutes, I'll turn the stage over to the people who will be organizing your grad party. First though, I need to say that our first priority is to keep our students safe. For that reason, we're proposing some changes this year.

"Last year, we had some concerns about alcohol," he continues. "We know that some of our graduating students are legally old enough to drink. But we need to make sure that nobody will be driving that night. So we're going to model this year's grad party on something called a 'Safe Grad.'"

"*Lame!*"

"*Oh my god!*"

Kids are calling out from all areas of the gym. Mr. Shah raises his hand to try to settle them down.

"Right now, I'm going to call on Mandy Mok and Diego Rodriguez. They are the student reps, and they will explain about Safe Grad. I expect you to keep an open mind about what they have to say."

Mandy steps up to the microphone. "Like Mr. Shah said, there will be some changes to the grad party this year. Just like other years, the party will happen the same night as the banquet. We'll get dressed up and our families will be taking pictures and feeling proud of us. That part will be fun," she says. "But then, we ditch the fancy clothes after dinner. And we party!"

The chant goes up around the gym. "*Par-ty, par-ty, par-ty!*"

Mandy smiles and waits out the crowd. "So there have to be a few rules," she says finally. "Like, first of all, none of the grade twelves will be allowed to drive that night. It doesn't matter if they've had anything to drink or not. Everyone who buys a ticket to attend Safe Grad will catch a bus at the school. The bus will take us to the party. Then we all take a bus back to the school afterward. Everyone will have a parent pick them up from school."

Mandy moves away from the microphone. Diego steps forward. He pushes his hair off his face and smiles a cute, crooked grin.

"Hey, everyone," he says. "I am Diego Rodriguez." He says his name with an accent. Like me, it sounds like Diego has a grandmother — probably a Spanish one — who he speaks another language with.

"I'm here to promise you," Diego says, "this will be the best grad party Ashton Heights has ever had." He waits for the cheering to subside. "Okay, we don't want outsiders to crash our party. So we are going to keep the location of the party top secret, even from you students. Parent volunteers will be confiscating phones before you get on the buses."

A big groan goes up from the grade twelves.

"Relax!" Diego says. "You'll get your phones back later! We'll just hold on to them while everyone's at the party. We don't want people using their phones' location services to direct anyone else to the party. And while the parent volunteers are getting your phones, they'll also be checking purses and bags for alcohol."

"Good luck with that one!" someone calls out.

A roar goes up around the gym again.

"Students who are eighteen years and older can bring in picture ID and a reasonable amount of alcohol a week before Safe Grad. The parent volunteers will label the unopened bottles with students' names and store them in a warehouse. Those students can collect their booze at the Safe Grad party.

"In other words," Diego says, "we know some people will drink that night. But nobody drives. Our goal is to keep everyone safe."

Diego steps aside for Mandy.

"And the last thing," she says as she takes the mic again, "we need more students to help out on the grad committee. So if you'd like to get involved, we hope you'll join us. Our next meeting is tomorrow at lunch in the Book Loft."

The Book Loft is where grade twelves go to really study and to work in groups. Nobody is allowed to use cell phones in there. So it's probably the best place for someone who's afraid of getting exposed — on social media or anywhere else. I catch myself thinking that

checking out a couple of meetings might be
safe. But then I shake my head. I know Mandy
is going to step up the pressure on me to join.
I have to stay strong.

I'm hardly to the door when Mandy
catches up with me.

"Hey, you were great," I say.

"Really?" Mandy grabs me in a hug.
"Thanks. So you'll join —"

I need to change the subject fast. And there
is something I want to know.

"By the way, Mandy," I say, "which guy
was Caprice fighting over this morning?"

"With Fatima?" Mandy comes to a full
stop beside me. "You don't know?"

"No. I've had my head down. Getting
caught up with classes and stuff."

"It's Diego," Mandy says.

"Seriously? But he seems like such a nice
guy."

"I know." Mandy shakes her head. "I don't
get it either."

At that moment, Diego steps through the gym doors behind us. We're close enough that I can hear his accent. I take in his plaid shirt, his slouchy blue jeans, and his cute, crooked grin. He looks so sweet.

But as I learned from Duncan, looks can be deceiving.

"Come on." I grab Mandy's arm and pull her along. "Let's get out of here."

Chapter 13

Suspended

I can tell before I'm even awake that our place is empty. Mom has switched to the opening shift at Starbucks. My classes don't start until 10:30, so I usually drop by the coffee shop after the morning rush. But this morning, I'm leaving our apartment extra early to make a phone call.

When I step inside the phone booth, the smell of piss and cigarettes makes my stomach twist. It will have to be a fast call.

"Mémère?" I say.

"Vienna, *chérie*! *Ça va*?"

"*Oui, ça va*. Everything is fine."

"*Merci, Dieu*. But I still don't even know where you are." Between thanking God and worrying about us, Mémère sounds close to tears.

"I know, Mémère. I'm sorry. *Désolée*," I say. "But things are going better."

I realize it's true. Mom is holding down her job and has given up drinking at home. I'm truly going to graduate. Still, I'm glad Mémère can't see our cramped little apartment. It's also good that she can't see the men leering at me as they circle the tavern near the pay phone.

"And Mom's job is going great," I say. "She works at a coffee shop. She's met some nice friends here too. She's doing better that way than I am."

I realize how that last part sounds. So I add a laugh at the end as though I was joking. Mémère doesn't have to know it's true.

"Sophie is making me proud. I wish —"
Mémére's voice trails off.

I know what she was going to say.
She wishes they hadn't fought about Mom
marrying Duncan. Mémère sounds so sad that
I hate to ask her my next question. But I need
to know.

"Has Duncan talked to you again,
Mémère?" As soon I mention Duncan, my
chin and my arm itch. I'm glancing around at
the dusty, littered sidewalk as though Duncan
might appear there at any second.

"*Non*," Mémère says. "*Mais il a beaucoup
de problèmes.*"

"He has a lot of problems?"

"*Oui*. At the hospital, they found he was
using drugs. I am following it on the internet.
Duncan had to do more drug tests, and they
were positive. Duncan has been —"

Mémère struggles to remember the word
in English, "— *suspendu*."

"Suspended?"

"*Oui.* He has lost his licence to be a pharmacist."

I wonder what he'll do instead. And maybe it means Kyla finally got her claws in him. Then again, maybe Kyla lost interest since he's no longer her boss.

It serves Duncan right. And anything that keeps him busy and in Toronto is better for Mom and me.

My whole body feels lighter. I'm still thinking about all of this when Mémère speaks up again.

"*Pardon?*" I ask.

"*Vous me manquez,*" she says. My eyes fill with tears. Mémère sounds so old and so sad.

"We miss you too, Mémère. And I don't want you to worry about us. We really are doing okay." Then an idea comes to me. "And I'm going to send you a picture so you can see for yourself. You watch the mail for it, okay?

"Right now, I need to go meet Mom at work. But I'll phone you again soon. *À bientôt.*"

"*À bientôt, chérie.*"

* * *

The morning staff at Starbucks — Mom, Salma, Ji-Won, and Ahmed — scramble to test out new drinks on me when I arrive. Today's offering is espresso with steamed milk and praline nuts crumbled over top. I'll definitely leave for school with a good caffeine buzz.

While I finish the latte and my muffin, ancient Mr. Christofi, in his suit with a little bowtie, pores over the newspaper. The same two men are arguing in the far corner in a language that Ahmed said is Turkish. I'm keeping an eye out for Yulia. Mom said she dropped by once and almost smiled when Mom made her a pumpkin-spice latte. I'd have to see that myself to believe it.

I get to school just in time for Business class. Lunch period is next. But after the heavy coffee drinks, muffins, and croissants that Mom and her barista friends slip me, I'm never hungry. That works well, because I avoid the cafeteria. It freaks me out that students are always snapping pictures of themselves and everyone around them. And Caprice is always there with the same friends who thought it was hilarious when Caprice told me to "move my ass" the first day of school.

So instead, I take off to the library. That would be perfect except once again, Fatima is there. Whenever I see Fatima, the panic I felt when Caprice was beating on her comes rushing back. Fatima sometimes tries to catch my eye, so I make sure to look the other way when I see her flitting around the bookshelves. I heave a sigh of relief as she disappears behind the stacks. She probably hangs out here for the same reasons that I do. Still, I wish she'd find another place to spend her lunch hour.

I'm getting my English notes from our locker when Mandy storms down the hall. The whole time, she's cursing under her breath.

"Hey, what's up?" I ask.

She doesn't answer me. As she turns to

stuff a file folder into the locker, the pages inside the folder fall out and slide across the tile floor.

"Here, I can help." I bend over to pick up the papers. We nearly bump heads.

"You know what?" Mandy says sharply. "We might as well just leave them there."

"Why?"

"Because it looks like this grad party isn't going to happen. How could they ditch on us?"

"What are you talking about? Who ditched on you?"

"Olivia Eto and Brody Lam." Mandy is waving her hands through the air. "For the last two weeks, Brody couldn't keep his hands off of Olivia. And she was practically sitting on his lap during the meetings. Talk about awkward. So when I heard they were going to a movie together on the weekend, I was like, good. Maybe they can make out *there* instead."

I grab the last few papers from the floor and close our locker.

"But the date was a total bomb," Mandy says with disgust. She has short legs, but I'm struggling to keep up with her. "And now they can't stand each other so they've ditched the grad committee. That leaves *me* to try to do everything. And it's just as my parents are telling me to quit the grad committee because of my grades."

"Oh no." I pause for a moment. "Do you think maybe you should quit?"

"No way!" Mandy comes to a sudden stop. "I'm not an academic genius like my brothers, Mr. Astro-Physicist and Mr. Chemistry Major. But I'm really good at planning events. I'm not just going to drop it." Mandy's whole body sags. "But I know my parents are going to give me tons of grief."

"I'm sorry, Mandy. That really sucks. I wish I could help but . . ."

Mandy spins around to face me. "You know," she says, "you can. We're seriously short on people. And you said you'd think about joining."

I scroll back through my mind. I maybe said that, but it was just to put her off.

Mandy continues. "Olivia and Brody were on the food and location team with me. There's no way I can finish everything on my own. So can you help me? Please?"

I'm opening my mouth to say "no." But then I think about how Mom has a bunch of new friends. Maybe it's a good idea for me to get involved with the Safe Grad after all.

"Please, Vienna?" Mandy's eyes are sparkling. "It'll be fun!"

"I'll think about it," I say. "But only if you don't ask me about it again today. I'll let you know tomorrow."

Mandy reaches over and gives me a hug. I know she's already counting on me. So now I just need to figure out if I'm ready to do this or not.

Chapter 14

Signing On

Mom is chopping vegetables when I burst in. She's not making much money, but now we have more dinner options than Kraft Dinner, Yulia's disgusting borscht, and the food Mom brings home from work.

"Hey, what's on the menu?" I ask.

"Chicken stir fry," Mom says. "It's one of Jasmine's recipes."

"Sounds good." I drop my books on the kitchen table. "There's something I want to tell you about."

I fill in Mom about the Safe Grad committee. I'm pacing around the kitchen. I worry that it's just one more thing that can go wrong. So I'm trying to sound really cool — like it isn't a big deal. But the more I explain to Mom, the more it hits me that I'd really like to do this.

"So it's really just about helping out Mandy," I say. "Because I don't know if I'll be going to the grad party at all."

Mom sets down the paring knife and faces me. "What are you talking about?" she asks. "Not going to your own grad party? Of course you're going."

I'm not sure how I feel about that. "Well, I'm passing everything. So it looks like I'll actually graduate." I pause. "But what if we can't afford to buy a dress or whatever?"

"We'll make it work somehow," Mom says. Tears are streaming down her face. "I want you to have a few fond memories to look back on from your last year of high school. Not just the pain that Duncan caused us."

"I know, Mom," I say. "And we're getting by, right?"

"We haven't had the luxury of *not* getting by." Mom reaches for a dishtowel and wipes her eyes. "But I have been thinking that our lives have been much too serious. You haven't had the chance to just enjoy being a kid. So before you graduate from high school and officially *aren't* a kid any longer, you need to do this. I know you'll be careful. So would you just go and have some fun for a change?"

I nod. "Thanks," I say.

The next day, Mandy thanks me and hugs me over and over again. I'm not used to being hugged this much and it's scaring me a bit. I need to rein in Mandy.

"Okay," I say. I hold my hands in front of

me to stop her moving in on me again.

"I get that you're happy. So what do I have to do at this meeting? I know it's up to us to get the food. And we need to find a place to have the party. Other than that, I'm completely clueless."

"You'll figure it out fast," she says. "Come on!"

I'm speed walking to keep up with her as we head upstairs to the Book Loft. We're soon crammed around a table. Diego is the only student I know by name. He's laughing with Ms. Nygard, the teacher rep on the committee, and some other student volunteers. He seems like a nice, friendly guy, just like Mandy said he is. It amazes me all over again that he's dating Caprice.

"So everyone, this is Vienna Fleury," Mandy says. "Vienna is going to help me. Together we're the food and venue team." She starts going around the table. "This is Trinh Luong and Montana Horvath. They're on for decorations and setup. Keltie Wong and Ty Hussein are doing games and entertainment. Stella Cherniak and Michael Kowalski are on the fundraising and ticket sales team. And Diego and Ms. Nygard are overseeing Safe Grad and setting up transportation to the party and back."

My head swims as I try to take it all in.

"Welcome to the Safe Grad committee, Vienna," Ms. Nygard says.

Everyone is looking at me. I remind myself to stop rubbing my chin as I force a smile.

"I'd like to start today's meeting by getting an update from the various teams," Ms. Nygard says. "Mandy, why don't you tell us what progress you've made with food and venue."

"I've talked to all the local grocery stores and bake shops," Mandy says. "Most of them will either donate food or sell it to us at a discount. The problem so far is the venue. We still don't have a place for the party.

Olivia and Brody were supposed to look into that. But then they quit the committee."

Some of the students groan.

"Don't worry," says Mandy. "Vienna and I will make some calls to see if we can find a place for the party."

The other teams give an update. But all I hear is that they need Mandy and me to hurry up and find a place for the party. Then they can finish their jobs too.

"There is one more thing I want to remind everyone of before we work in our teams," Ms. Nygard says. "We are keeping ticket prices as low as possible. Even so, if you hear of any students who feel they can't go to their own grad party because of costs, please let me know. I'll speak with those students privately. We'll make sure they get to attend."

My face burns. If I decide to go to the grad party, I'm pretty sure I'll be one of those people who can't afford to be there.

We break off into our teams. Mandy and I step into the office at the back of the Book Loft.

"I have a list here. I'll make the first phone call," Mandy says. "You're on for the next one."

I swallow hard and nod. I listen to Mandy and do my best to memorize everything she says. It'll be my turn next. My stomach is churning. But I remind myself that after everything Mom and I have been through, this should be easy.

Chapter 15

Trouble

"Any luck finding a place for the party?" Trinh asks.

"Nothing so far," I say. "We're still —"

"Our volunteers are ready to start selling tickets," Montana says. "But before we print the tickets, we need to know how much the rental will cost. Until then, we don't know how much to charge for the tickets."

Ms. Nygard joins them. "I was just talking to the bus company," she says. "They need to know the distance to the party venue so that —"

Mandy takes a deep breath. "We haven't found a place yet."

The scars on my chin and my arm burn. They always do at the first sign of trouble. I'm keeping my face turned down. I'm shuffling through the papers in the file folder when a business card drops onto the floor.

I pick it up and read it. "Trent Timmins, Event Coordinator. What about him?"

"I think Brody's family knows Trent," Mandy says. "That's why the card is there."

"That's right," Ms. Nygard says. "We didn't pursue it because he would probably charge a lot of money. The more work we do ourselves, the lower the ticket price for the students."

I'm about to throw it away. But I see Montana's crossed arms and the scowl on Trinh's face. I make a fast decision. "I'm going to give Trent a call," I say. "He might at least have some suggestions for us."

"Trent Timmins here."

"Hi," I say, "I'm phoning from Ashton Heights High School. We're planning our grad party. We're looking for a venue for June twenty-ninth that's a one-hour drive outside of Edmonton."

"I know several venues that are about that far away. How many guests?"

"About two hundred." I hear Trent flipping through some papers.

"Last year," he says, "I planned an outdoor wedding at a venue that might work for you. The main building holds more than two hundred people. It has a nice indoor kitchen."

"It sounds great," I say. "We want to set up a games area and a dance floor. So we'll need a large building with different areas. Either indoors or outdoors will do."

Then I remember what Ms. Nygard said about Trent charging a lot of money. "And there's one other thing," I say. "We probably can't afford your usual rates. We need to keep ticket prices low for our students. So if you could maybe offer a discount . . ."

My voice trails off. I've been trying to sound official. I don't want him to think I'm just some dumb kid who's planning the first high-school party she's ever attended. I mean, that's totally the case. But he doesn't need to know that. I think about how certain I sounded when I bought the bus tickets to Edmonton. Can I convince Trent that I actually know what I'm doing?

Just as I'm sure he's hung up on me, Trent speaks up. "I appreciate that you guys are in a bind. But I know of only one place that works for a reduced budget. It's more than an hour outside of Edmonton. And it's not really on my list yet, because I haven't tried it out. So I can't get my usual catering and decorating companies."

"I guess we could do our own set up and source our own food," I say. It's a bluff. We were already going to handle that ourselves. I've become good at putting on a strong act.

"Okay, I could offer you a special deal on a new venue I'd like to start using for my events," Trent says. "Call it a trial run."

He quotes me a price. It sounds too good to be true. I don't want to rush into this.

"So what's the real story here, Trent?" I ask. "Why so low?"

"Well, it's not a banquet hall. The owner used to run a horseback riding school there."

"So it's a riding arena?"

"Yes. But before you ask, it does *not* smell like a barn. It's been fully cleaned. The arena is big enough for a food and games area. The concrete pad where people used to park their horse trailers would be perfect for a dance floor."

I'm jotting down information. Mandy, Diego, and Ms. Nygard are reading my notes over my shoulder. When I write down the rate, they all give me a thumbs-up.

"Okay, we can work with that," I say. "We'd like to book it."

Mandy's squeals are so loud I can hardly hear Trent.

"I can email you a contract this afternoon," he says.

Mandy and Diego start cheering. Within seconds, the whole Book Loft knows what happened.

Ms. Nygard is beaming. "Good job, Vienna," she says. "I've been worried. We're late booking a venue. I was afraid we wouldn't find anything at this point. I think you just saved the grad party."

"Finally!" Diego says. "Finally, we're getting this party underway!"

He grabs me and gives me a tight hug. I didn't see it coming and I cling to him to keep myself from tumbling to the carpet. Before he lets me go, Diego makes sure I have my balance.

I'm looking around me while I catch my

breath. Then my heart nearly stops. Caprice is standing just inside the door. If looks could kill, I'd be dead.

In an excited voice, Diego explains to Caprice how I just got us a place for the party. As everyone leaves the Book Loft, she turns back. As she glares at me, I picture her beating on Fatima. A tremor starts at my knees then works all the way up my body.

Oh my god! How much trouble have I just landed myself in?

✳ ✳ ✳

With Safe Grad pretty much planned, I've gone back to hiding out in the library. I study for final exams and pretend I don't notice Fatima. Part of me wants to tell her that I'm sorry I couldn't help her when Caprice was beating her up. But I can't just walk up to her and say that.

It's a relief when Mandy and Diego call another meeting.

Mandy and I are almost at the Book Loft when we hear shouts echoing down the hall.

"What the f —" says the girl's voice.

"Can you keep your voice down?" the guy's voice asks.

"Keep my voice down? After what you —"

"Look, I'm trying but —"

"But *what*, you dick!"

"But you're not helping."

"Helping? I'm supposed to be *helping* you? While you're dumping me for some bitch you're probably screwing?"

"Caprice, that's nuts. I'm not sleeping with anyone."

Caprice is screaming with rage. She runs straight into me as she turns the corner.

When Caprice sees that it's me, she says, "This is because of *you!*"

Mandy grabs my arm. "Let's go."

My legs are shaking as we step into the Book Loft.

"We'd better start without Diego,"

Ms. Nygard says. "Let's hear some updates."

"We signed the contract with Trent for the venue." I'm fighting to keep my voice steady. "And we paid him the deposit."

"We'll give him the final payment the night of the party," Mandy adds.

I don't take in the updates from everyone else. I wonder if Diego managed to calm down Caprice. I think back to Caprice's attack on Fatima. I know who she's going after next.

* * *

When the meeting ends Mandy asks me, "Did you buy your grad dress yet?"

I shake my head. I haven't told Mandy that my main concerns are that it is "cheap like borscht" and that the sleeves cover the scar on my arm. "Don't worry. I'll find something."

"Damn right you will!" Mandy pulls her laptop out of her backpack. "We're going to check out the grad dress page."

"The *what*?"

Mandy rolls her eyes. "It's called 'Grad Dresses of Ashton Heights.' It's where you post a picture of yourself wearing your grad dress. The idea is that nobody else is supposed to buy the same one."

Mandy scrolls down. We're soon checking out the long dresses and the short dresses, the sweet ones and the sexy ones.

"Trinh looks gorgeous in coral," I say.

"I know," Mandy says. "And check out Keltie's strapless."

I take a closer look. "Pretty, but dangerous," I say. "It's a wardrobe malfunction waiting to happen. And there's Caprice —" My eyes grow wide. "Oh my god! Check out the comment below her picture."

Mandy reads it out loud. "*God help the bitch who shows up at grad with my ex.*"

Chapter 16

This New Life

"So, your *examens*," Mémère says, "you passed all of them?"

"Yes, my exams all went well." My eyes fill with tears. I think back all those months to when Mom and I first arrived in Edmonton. I hardly dared to hope that I'd come away with a high school diploma. But it's going to happen. Tomorrow night.

"Do you have a date for your party?" Mémère asks. "*Un garçon spécial?*"

A special boy. Definitely not!

"*Non*, Mémère. I helped plan the party,"
I say, "with some friends." *Friends. I like how
that word sounds.* "So I'll have some jobs to do
during the party."

"*Eh bien*, I hope you get to enjoy yourself
too."

"I definitely will," I say. "I promise."

"*Et Sophie?*" As usual, Mémère's voice fills
with sadness when she mentions Mom.

"She's doing well," I say. "She really likes
her job." Then I quickly add, "And she's working
full-time. So she's pretty busy. I wish you could
be here with us tomorrow night, Mémère."

As soon as the words are out of my mouth,
guilt washes over me. Mémère still doesn't
know where "here" actually is. I wonder if I'll
ever be able to tell her.

Then I remember something else. "Did
you get the picture I sent you?"

"*Non. Pas encore.*"

"Not yet? I sent it almost two weeks ago."

I think back to when I coaxed Mom into a photo booth with me at the mall. She was surprised because I'm usually so tight with our money. I didn't tell her why we were doing it. But it felt good cutting one of the pictures off the strip and slipping it into an envelope. I sent it to Mémère — without a return address, of course.

"I'm sure it will arrive any day," Mémère says.

"*D'accord*," I agree. "Mémère, I need to go. I'll phone you soon to tell you all about graduation."

As I hang up, I wonder what is happening back in Toronto. Back in Duncan's world. Whatever it is, I hope it's keeping his mind off Mom and me.

Then I decide to put that out of my mind, because tomorrow night, I have a grad party to enjoy.

I thought Mandy would have a heart attack when I didn't buy a grad dress until last week. I didn't tell her I bought the first dress I tried on at the consignment store. It fit *and* the sleeves were long enough to cover the scar on my arm. It's only as I'm getting dressed for grad that I realize how much I love it. The shimmery emerald fabric hugs my hips then flares out and skims the floor.

I grab my bag with my clothes for the party after the banquet, then Mom and I head out the door together.

"Such a special day." I can hear the tears at the edge of Mom's voice. "I wish your father were alive to see it."

"I know," I say as we walk up the front entrance to the school. "So much has happened since —"

"*Oh my god!*"

"I'd know that shriek anywhere," I say. We stop and wait for Mandy to catch up with us.

"Diego's going to pass out when he sees you in that dress!" Mandy says.

I check around me to see if anyone heard her. Whew, nobody else is looking our way!

"Diego?" Mom asks.

"He's just a guy on the grad committee," I say. "Mandy's imagining things. And you," I turn toward Mandy, "you look gorgeous!"

Mandy is glowing. Her turquoise-blue gown has gathers up the side and crisscrossed fabric at the neckline. I hug her carefully so I don't mess up her hair and makeup. Then the three of us fall into the stream of graduates and their families going into the gym.

"This way," Mandy says. "I sent my parents on ahead. They're saving seats for us."

Except for the faintest smell of sweat, you could forget that this is our school gym. Balloons, flowers, and streamers cover the room.

Mom and I join Mandy's parents at a table in the middle of the gym. Nadine and Vic are both cute, bouncy little people like Mandy. They snap dozens of pictures of Mandy and me. Mandy alone, me alone, Mandy and me together.

Nadine and Vic finally set down their cameras. We settle in to watch the slideshow that's playing on the wall. Each slide has a student's yearbook photo next to a baby picture. School photos were taken before we moved to Edmonton, so I don't have one of those. A few weeks ago, the decoration committee asked the grads to bring in a baby picture to scan for the slideshow. I almost didn't ask Mom. I was sure she wouldn't have one. I was surprised when she'd pulled a ragged baby picture out of her wallet. In the photo, I'm sitting on Santa's knee. I'm wearing a green velvet dress and white tights. Little pigtails poke out from each side of my head. We all laugh when it appears on the screen.

The slideshow runs through a few times before Mr. Shah announces that the grads need to line up outside the gym doors. Mandy and I are making our way there when someone speaks up behind us.

"So green has always been your colour?"

I blush and turn around. It's Diego, who looks extra cute in a slightly too-big suit jacket, a pair of black jeans, and sneakers.

"You mean my baby picture." I finally find my voice. "I left the white tights and little pigtails at home tonight."

As we wait in line, teachers are directing us to join the grad parade in twos and threes. Mandy and I are almost at the door when Diego steps between us and offers each of us an arm. So that's how we enter the gym.

I look over at Mom. The last time she looked this happy was six years ago, before Dad was diagnosed with cancer. Mom raises her eyebrows when she notices Diego with Mandy and me. I hope she's not expecting any big news about him later. She'll be in for a letdown.

With cameras flashing all around us, the grads circle the edge of the gym. Then we join our families again at our tables. A smile has spread all over my face. A warm glow radiates through my whole body as I think about this new life that Mom and I have built. It feels like a miracle. And as the evening stretches out before me in my mind, I'm sure it will be the best night of my life.

Chapter 17

"Party! Party!"

"Who was that boy you walked into the gym with?" Mom asks.

"Oh, that's Diego," I say. "A guy Mandy and I worked with on Safe Grad."

I smile and glance around the room. But my eyes land on Caprice, who's scowling from two tables over. The glow I was feeling vanishes on the spot.

Mandy follows my gaze. Then she leans in closer to me. "Caprice is *so* not ruining the grad party for us."

"You're right," I say. "We've earned this."

Mr. Shah is calling table numbers to line up at the buffet. It's finally our turn. But even though I'm hungry, I hardly taste the salad, the buns, the two kinds of pasta, the veggies, and the vanilla cake.

The plates are almost cleared away when Mr. Shah steps up to the microphone again. "I'd like the graduates to line up in alphabetical order, just as we practised earlier today. Have your name card ready to hand to Mrs. Singh. She will introduce you before you cross the stage."

Outside in the hall, I shuffle from side to side as I wait for my name to be called.

"Vienna Fleury."

Oh my god, oh my god, oh my god. This is really happening! How I wish you were here, Dad and Mémère.

Mr. Shah hands me my diploma. It feels like a major victory that I don't cry in front of everyone. Back at our table, Mom's eyes are shining. I look away fast so we both don't start.

Once we've all crossed the stage, Mr. Shah talks about how proud he is of the grads and their families. It isn't long before the chant starts building. Soon it fills the gym.

"*Party! Party!*"

Mr. Shah waits it out. "I understand a party is going to follow the banquet. But first, we have a tradition here at Ashton Heights. Please take the floor for the annual dance with the grads and their parents."

When the music starts, I grab Mom. We shuffle at the edge of the dance floor. Mom is doing a sweet, jerky little circle. I can tell she's spending as little time as possible on her sore leg.

"I need to tell you again how proud I am of you," Mom says.

"Thanks, Mom. Yeah, it's been . . ."

I can't find the words to tell her how proud

I am of her. Proud of her for leaving Toronto and not looking back. So I just hug her extra tightly until the song finishes.

"This concludes the formal part of the evening," Mr. Shah says. "Now it's time for the announcement that our grads have been waiting for."

He doesn't get to make the announcement though. The roar that erupts throughout the gym is deafening.

"*Party! Party!*"

Everyone rushes from the gym. The change rooms are packed with bodies as we whip off our grad clothes and pull on jeans and t-shirts.

I work my way back to Mom by the gym doors.

"Have fun." Mom gives me a big smile. She takes my grad dress and heels, and my diploma.

My stomach twitches with excitement as Mandy and I join the crowds at the school buses. All the cell phones are taken and our bags checked. Then we pile onto the buses. The hard vinyl seats and the smell of partially eaten lunches in the garbage container at the back remind me of something. I think back to the broken state Mom and I were in when we left Toronto on the bus all those months ago.

I'm trying to take calm, even breaths when the seat lurches. My heart races as someone grabs it then slams down behind us.

"Hey, you two!" Diego says.

Mandy laughs. Once my heart stops hammering, I force a laugh too.

The bus whizzes down the highway then along a series of bumpy gravel roads. We finally drive through a gate.

Diego leans forward. "Welcome to Safe Grad," he says.

"The moment we've been waiting for," Mandy says.

I nod and jump from my seat. Then I follow the jostling pack of new grads away to the party.

＊ ＊ ＊

The kids around the "Booze Claim Tent"
are jostling and pushing as the music blares
around us. Keltie and Ty have set up a games
area with card tables and board games.
Squeals of laughter are coming from where
a bunch of kids are already playing Twister.
Noemi, a girl from my French class, is getting
tangled up with Ty. Her butt is practically in
his face — which Ty doesn't seem to mind —
as they tumble to the floor.

Keltie bounces over to us. "I figured
Twister would be a hit." Then she whispers,
"Just wait till everyone's had some more
drinks."

Mandy and I watch for a few minutes
before we go inside to set up the food area.
Table legs clatter against the concrete floor as
we line them up. Then we pull out the chips,
pretzels, popcorn, and other snack food.

"Done, I think," Mandy says.

"It looks good," Ms. Nygard says. "Now go have some fun. I'll need your help again later, but you're free until 12:30."

We step outside the main building. People are wandering around in groups. Some have joints and beer or vodka coolers in their hands. A couple of people pretend to cover it up when they see us.

"I'm glad it's not the grad committee's job to monitor that," Mandy says.

"Me too." The music is too loud for Mandy to notice how choked my voice sounds. I can't think too much about drinking or smoking. Given Duncan's usual addicted state, the smell of booze and drugs is tied to him in my mind.

I push that thought out of my head. I refuse to let Duncan ruin even one more minute of my life — especially tonight. So when Neal and Diego call us over to the dance floor, I pull Mandy along with me. We start dancing under the trees.

I usually feel awkward and self-conscious on the dance floor. But tonight something kicks in and I just dance. Trinh and Montana have joined us too. For the first time ever, it feels like my arms and legs weren't just stuck onto my body to embarrass the hell out of me. Diego's hair tumbles over his forehead. He dances in crazy jags of energy that make everyone laugh.

"Are you always this much fun?" I ask.

Diego's smile suddenly disappears as he looks across the dance floor. I see Caprice glaring at us from the other side.

God help the bitch who shows up at grad with my ex. I shudder as the words run through my mind.

"I wasn't always this much fun," Diego says. "I had a few lapses." Then he looks at me. His smile comes back. "But I am now."

Chapter 18

Caught

When I finally check the time, I can't believe how late it is.

"Mandy, we've got to get out the desserts."

"Okay," Mandy groans. "Let's just throw them on the table super fast."

Outside the building, a crowd of students is waiting by the massive grills where parent volunteers are barbecuing hamburgers and hot dogs. Two parents suddenly break away from the group. I soon see why. A girl with purple hair and her sobbing friend are puking up whatever they drank into plastic bags in their hands. The parents lead the girls away to the early buses to take them back to the school. Their party is cut short.

"Ew, nasty," Mandy says. "Let's go!"

We dash into the building where Ms. Nygard is waiting. We refill the platters of buns, meats, cheeses, and lettuce. At the far end of the table, kids are making sandwiches.

I pull out tray after tray of fruit, cookies, brownies, tarts, and slices of cake. Mandy sets out the toppings for make-your-own ice cream sundaes. I rummage through the cardboard boxes under the table.

"We're out of bowls," I say.

"There's another package in my car," Ms. Nygard says. She hands me her keys. "Can you and Mandy go get them? My car is the red Corolla by the back gate."

We're stepping away when a table leg collapses. Mandy grabs the edge of the table.

A tray of cookies slides onto the floor but she manages to save everything else. Mandy holds on to the table as Ms. Nygard rushes over to help.

"Go ahead to the car, Vienna," Mandy says. "I'll be there in a minute."

I step outside and weave through the pine trees at the edge of the property. The streetlamp in the parking area flickers. I'm opening the back gate when a voice calls out behind me.

"Having a good time with my ex?" Venom drips from Caprice's voice. She's swaying and she smells like beer.

Oh, no! My throat tightens.

"I warned you," she says. "I *warned* you! He told me you're not having sex. But why else would he ditch me?"

My heart is hammering as she shoves me outside the fence. I land on my hands and knees in the gravel by Ms. Nygard's car.

"Caprice!" Mandy is puffing as she catches

up to us. "Leave her alone! Nobody is here with your ex. That's just dumb!"

Mandy is about half Caprice's size. But right now, she's making herself almost as big as Caprice using pure attitude.

"And what were you thinking with that post on the grad dresses page?" Mandy says. "'*God help the bitch who shows up at grad with my ex.*' Seriously, Caprice?"

Mandy is accenting her words with jabs of her finger toward Caprice's face. To my surprise, Caprice is actually listening to Mandy. She is even backing up. I would never have expected that.

I decide to follow Mandy's lead. "And you know something else?" I say as I stand up. "You *still* owe Fatima a huge apology for what you did to her."

I brush the gravel from my hands and knees. I'm bending over to pick up Ms. Nygard's keys when the voice that haunts my nightmares rings out behind me.

"Hey, sugar."

Oh god! It can't be! I turn around.

"How —?" I'm shaking my head.

Duncan shrugs his shoulders. "I followed the bus from your school. I kept a discreet distance, of course."

He leers at me. Even in the dim light, I can see his eyes are bright red. His boozy breath catches me square in the face. I throw up on the spot.

* * *

Moments later, I hear screaming. I only realize that I'm the one doing the screaming when Duncan slaps me. It feels like a swarm of wasps just stung the side of my face. My body spirals sideways and I'm on the ground.

"*What the hell?*" Caprice says.

Everything seems to happen in slow motion. Mandy is rushing toward me. Duncan reaches into his jacket and pulls out a gun. Mandy's feet skid in the gravel as she stops short.

I remember when Duncan bought the gun. To protect the pharmacy from drug addicts, he said. I should have known that one day Duncan would pull it on me.

"You'll have to wait your turn," Duncan says to Caprice. "I'm not done talking to my long-lost stepdaughter yet."

Duncan pulls me to my feet. "That was a nice picture you sent your grandmother," he says. "That ugly scar on your chin showed up real nice. I thought your mom looked a little worse for wear." He laughs. "I'll bet she's missing me."

How does he know about the picture?

"The Edmonton postmark on the envelope made it real easy to track you down."

Shit! A postmark? That was the first time I'd ever sent anything through the mail. I didn't know it would have "Edmonton" marked on it! I thought I had covered our tracks by not writing a return address on the envelope.

"Vienna? Mandy?" I hear Diego calling from the other side of the gate.

"Diego, run!" Mandy yells. "He's got a gun!"

Duncan lunges forward and cracks Mandy on the side of her head with the gun. I scream as she drops to the ground. It makes no sense that my friend — probably the best friend I've ever had — is unconscious. And it's all because of my messed-up family and me.

Please be okay, Mandy! The words race through my mind over and over again.

"Time to clear out of here," Duncan says. His hot, sickening breath on my face nearly makes me puke again. He holds out his hand. "Car keys."

I remember how Mandy and I stood up to Caprice just minutes ago. "No way!" I say.

"You'll do what I tell you to, bitch!" Duncan tears the keys out of my hand. Then he points the gun at Caprice and me. "You two, lift your little friend into the front seat."

Caprice looks over to see what I'm going to do. With the gun pointing at us at close range, we don't have any choice. I grab Mandy under her arms. Caprice takes her feet. As we shuffle sideways with Mandy between us, I wish there was something I could do. All I want is to rewind the evening. To go back to the time when the only danger was Caprice.

"I don't have all day." Duncan kicks at me and my knees nearly buckle.

When we finally get Mandy into the passenger seat, Duncan kicks the door shut.

"Vienna, you and this one," he points at Caprice, "get in the backseat. Now!"

Once we're in the car, Duncan revs the engine. My head thuds against the back of the seat as he spins out. My stomach gives a massive thud too. I wish I could do something heroic. I even want to try to save Caprice. I never would have imagined that even five minutes ago.

Then the question pushes its way into my head. *Why didn't I kill Duncan when I had the chance?* As I sit frozen in the backseat of Ms. Nygard's car, I know that this is my fault. I couldn't do it that last night in Toronto. So Mandy and Caprice have been pulled into Duncan's ugliness too.

Duncan's words are running through my head. *You'll do what I tell you to!*

Duncan always used fear to keep me captive. It's just like how he's holding me, Mandy, and Caprice hostage now. So tonight, I have to do better. But how? And what if I can't?

"I never thought my grad party would end like this." Caprice's voice pulls me back into the moment. "Hey, Vienna's father. Any chance you can let me out of here?" She's slurring her words.

Duncan doesn't say anything for a long moment. My stomach is clenching and unclenching. I know something that

Caprice doesn't: nobody gets the last word on Duncan.

But then he proves me wrong — sort of. He doesn't say anything at all. Instead, he lifts the gun and points it at Mandy. She's still slumped over in the passenger seat. I feel like I just got plunged into ice water. I elbow Caprice and shake my head from side to side. I need her to get the hint and shut up for once.

But what if she doesn't? What if she keeps mouthing off at Duncan? What if she taunts him until he follows through on his threat?

Oh, god! What then?

Chapter 19

Falling

Thankfully Caprice shuts up.

"Young lady," Duncan says to Caprice, "did I hear you right? You know, when you said that my stepkid is sleeping with your ex?"

He doesn't wait for an answer. "Well, sugar," he says to me. "Didn't you grow up to be quite the fine lady."

I close my eyes against the nausea that sweeps over me.

"What do you want?" I finally ask.

"To take my family home with me."
Duncan drawls out the words. "Back where
they belong. Where I can keep an eye on
them and everyone can see that I'm in
control, despite how screwed up my wife and
stepdaughter are. I'm sure your mother will
also testify that the drugs I took were for her.
So here's how this is going to work. You're
going to take me to my lovely wife."

I'm shaking my head again and again.
"Not a chance!" A police siren wails in the
distance and Duncan steps even harder on the
gas. The car weaves along the twisty dirt road.
The heavy gravel at the edge almost draws it
into the ditch. Police lights flash behind us
and my heart leaps. Then Duncan does the last
thing I expect. He slows down. He turns on
the lights inside the car.

When the police get closer, he opens his
window and holds his gun outside of it.

"Stand up, ladies! *Now!*" He glances into
the rearview mirror. "The cops might as well

see I have a carload of girls here. And a gun."

Caprice and I raise ourselves off the back seat as much as we can. The lights behind us grow fainter.

"Looks like they got the message," Duncan says. "You two can sit down again. And you, Miss Vienna, are going to tell me where to find my wife."

"I'm not telling you a thing!"

"Suit yourself." He points the gun at Mandy's head.

Oh no! Oh god!

I stammer out an address. "One-fifty-three Jasper Avenue."

Duncan laughs. "You've never been the smartest kid. Maybe you mixed up a few numbers. Let's see if you have some ID in that purse."

The car swerves as he reaches back and grabs my purse. He pulls at it until the strap breaks from around me.

I press my fists against my mouth to hold

back the scream. I've just remembered what's inside — the paper where Jerome wrote Yulia's address. *Our* address.

Duncan straightens the wheel. But just as it looks like he's heading for the highway, he turns back into the woods. Low-hanging tree branches swat at the windshield. My heart races as we swerve past the edge of the ravine. The headlights glance off the ground where it drops off on the passenger side.

Duncan pulls the car to a stop. He gets out and opens the passenger door. Then he points the gun at Caprice. "Help me lift this one out," he says to her.

Caprice steps out of the car. I'm alone in the backseat.

Mandy moans and stirs when Duncan tugs on her arm. He grunts as he tosses her over the edge of the ravine. I scream to block out the sound of Mandy rolling down the hill, her body slamming against trees and rocks on the way down.

Duncan clearly didn't need Caprice's help. I just have time to wonder why he wanted her out in the open when I get my answer. Duncan spins around and gives Caprice a massive push over the edge too.

Oh no! Mandy — and now Caprice too!

The headlights cast an eerie glow around the car. I remember all the times Duncan held me paralyzed with fear. I know he's counting on that again tonight. I can't let it happen.

As Duncan drops back into the driver's seat, I slide out the back door. I jump down into the thick bushes. I don't care where I go, as long as I'm beyond Duncan's reach. Police sirens shriek into the night. Duncan does a bellow of rage when he realizes he's alone in the car. And now, he does the only thing he can do. He roars away. Gravel sprays out behind Ms. Nygard's red car.

I'm trying to stop myself from tumbling down the ravine. But I was moving fast when I bolted from the car. The ground keeps falling away below me. Branches tear at my face and my hair and my hands. My skin scrapes against rocks and roots as I bump and roll down the hill. Finally, I crash to a stop against a boulder. My head bangs against it.

A moment later, the pain explodes in a hot, sick wave. The thought of trying to move hurts too much. I can't do it. But then I picture Duncan using that slip of paper in my purse to find Mom.

I have to get back up on the road. I need to flag down a car. I try to stand up but my legs won't hold me.

Through the fog in my head, I realize that the whole time we were driving, not a single car passed us. My heart sinks further.

With Duncan gone, I finally dare to speak. "Mandy? Caprice?"

Something rattles in the bushes below me. I start crawling in that direction. I try not to cry out as flashes of pain light up inside my head. I stifle moans when I bash my knee into a rock or when branches poke my face and eyes. I'm slipping further down with every movement. As I get deeper into the gulley, the darkness is making me even dizzier.

"Vienna?"

"Oh, thank god!" I sob. "Mandy, I need you to keep talking so I can get to you, okay?"

She groans. Then she murmurs something.

"What did you say?" I ask.

"Phone."

"I know." I can't stop crying. "I don't have one either."

"I. Do." I can tell her teeth are gritted against the pain.

"What? You still have your phone?"

I keep inching closer until I'm beside Mandy. My hand finally finds her arm. I lay my head down on the dead leaves and the sticks around us as I take her hand.

"I don't know where Caprice is," I say.

Fresh tears bubble to the surface. I would

never have guessed that Mandy would be safer with Caprice as a friend than with me.

But I have to push that thought out of my head. Because — what was it?

I remember now. "You brought your phone?"

"Um-hmm. Ms. Nygard said not to tell." Long pauses hang between her words. "She was nervous. Because our first Safe Grad. Said to bring mine — just in case."

I lift my head slightly. "So give me the phone," I say.

"Can't." Mandy's voice is groggy. It sounds like she's about to fall asleep. I don't think that's a good sign.

"Where is it?"

She doesn't answer me. I shake her shoulder. "Mandy, please stay with me. I'm afraid to be alone out here. The phone. I need you to give me the phone."

Mandy takes a deep, ragged breath. "Fell out." Then she settles back.

"Do you think it fell out down here?" I ask.

Her answer is just a murmur. I don't know if she even heard me. And I'm afraid to leave Mandy's side. If she falls asleep — or worse — I don't know if I'll be able to find her again.

But the phone is our only hope. For me, Mandy, Caprice. And for Mom. I crawl on hands and knees, sweeping with my scraped, bleeding hands as I move up toward the road. I want to hurry and cover more ground. But what if I miss the phone?

"Mandy." My head is throbbing and every muscle aches. I'd forgotten it was possible to hurt this much. "I can't find it." I choke the words out.

"Can't find what?" The voice is barely a whisper.

It's Caprice. I want to go to her but I'm afraid to veer off course.

"Caprice, help me find Mandy's phone."

"I can't," she sobs. "I can't move my leg."
All of Caprice's swagger has been knocked out
of her. I miss it.

I want to say something comforting. But
a wall of pain tightens around me. It hurts too
much to think of speaking or moving at all.

So instead, I think of someone else
moving one painful limb, then another.
Someone inching forward on hands and knees
until something has been picked up and
numbers pressed. I'm pretty sure I hear the
words "*please help*." Then the pain crowds it
all out and everything turns black.

Chapter 20

Safe

I open my eyes. There is whiteness and lights and beeps all around me. My eyes are too heavy to take everything in.

"Vienna. Vienna?"

I drag my eyes open again. A rectangle — almost like a computer screen — appears before me. Then a face appears at the edge of it.

"Mom?" My voice is dry and crackly like tissue paper.

"You're safe now, *chérie*."

"What?"

My mind lumbers over a tangle of memories. Driving in a red car. Then driving in something else. And hurting. And wanting all the movement and voices to just stop.

"Your friends are safe too."

"Mandy?"

"Yes," Mom says. "And Caprice too."

"What about —?" Something else is tugging at the back of my mind. I can't quite get there.

Then I remember. My body tenses and I cry out against the pain.

"Duncan."

"The police are waiting to arrest him," Mom takes a deep breath, "if he wakes up. Duncan crashed the car trying to get away from the police. It rolled down the ravine. He's been unconscious ever since."

I'm trying to process Mom's words. "So it's over?" I whisper.

"It's over." Tears are sliding down Mom's

face. "He can't hurt us anymore."

I shift toward her on the pillow. Then I wish I hadn't. Pain shoots through my head.

"Stay still," Mom says. "You need to rest."

"You too," I mumble.

"*Oui*," she says. "I'm going to go home to try to sleep. Do you need anything else?"

"Yes," I say. "I need you to phone Mémère."

"*D'accord*," Mom says. "I will. You've made all the phone calls you need to for now. That call you made on Mandy's cell phone saved all three of you. You were all in shock. Without your call, the police likely wouldn't have found you in time."

I vaguely remember Mandy's cell phone in someone's hand and numbers getting pressed. No one else was there except for the three of us. And Mandy and Caprice were too hurt to move.

It must have been me who made that phone call.

I'm trying to wrap my fuzzy brain around that thought. A nurse with blue glasses and a soft smile gives me something for the pain. Then time does a crazy twist on me. I have no idea how long I sleep.

* * *

Mom stays home with me for the week after I leave the hospital. We talk and we cry. Then we cry and we talk some more. I tell Mom about how I'd wanted to kill Duncan our last night in Toronto. I tell her how I'd felt guilty for not finishing him off. That triggers more tears from both of us. It's probably better after all that I don't have Duncan's death on my conscience.

Now that the school year is over, Mandy drops by for hours every day. And Mom picked up a cheap cell phone for me, so we've been texting a lot. I've even texted with Caprice. In a crazy way, Safe Grad brought the most unlikely people together.

My scrapes and bruises are healing well. Still, Mom doesn't want me to leave the house. I remind her that the yearbook people want a group picture of the Safe Grad committee.

The minute I walk in the school, I wonder if I've made a mistake. Summer school has started, so there are more kids around than I expected. The story of what happened at Safe Grad came out in the news. They wrote about Mom and me moving across the country to escape Duncan. Because I'm still underage for a few more weeks, they couldn't use my name. Still, everyone knows who it is. Today they're all staring at my bruised face, my neck brace, and my scratched hands and arms.

Even people who never talked to me before try to chat with me. I get that they're curious. But after working so hard to keep from being noticed, the attention makes my head hurt even more.

In some ways, it feels good having all the secrets lifted off of my shoulders. But the one thing I haven't told anyone, except for Mandy, is my old last name. I hated giving up Dad's last name when I came to Edmonton. The name Bauer was tied to the happiest, earliest years I had with both my parents. I might go back to using it again. But for now, Fleury feels good.

I'm just inside the school doors when Mandy appears. Her right arm is in a cast. The purple bruise on her forehead is turning yellow at the edges.

"This way," she says. "They're doing the picture in the library instead of the Book Loft. That way none of us has to tackle the stairs."

Most of the Safe Grad committee is already in the library. Theo, the photographer, has set up chairs for the group shot. He's trying to arrange everyone when the library door bursts open.

"Who the hell scheduled the photo shoot here?" Caprice swings into the room on her crutches. After everything that happened, we invited Caprice to be an honorary member of the Safe Grad committee and to join us for the yearbook photo.

"I thought we were doing this in the Book Loft," she says. "I've been up there looking for everyone. And since the regular elevator's broken, I had to take the service elevator. It was like I was a damn garbage bin or something."

Warmth spreads throughout my face and chest. I can't believe I'm happy to see Caprice getting her bounce back. Caprice had to enlist a bunch of people to help carry her stuff around for her. So her broken leg has helped her work on her social skills. Maybe I'm wrong about this, but it seems like some of Caprice's rough edges got worn off in the fall down into the gulley.

Theo insists that Mandy, Caprice, and I sit front row and centre. He wants our casts and crutches and neck braces to show up well. He's about to start when Ms. Nygard dashes into the library.

"I'm so sorry," she says. She starts to cry when she sees Mandy and me. "I had no idea what I was getting you girls into when I asked you to get those bowls from the car."

We give her a careful hug. She looks so sad that I start to cry too.

Trinh and Montana reach down from the row behind us to hug us. "Are you guys okay?" they ask.

"I think so." Ms. Nygard and I dab at our faces.

"Good, then quit messing with the group shot," Ty says.

"Yeah," Diego adds. "We don't need mascara stains and red eyes in the picture."

Caprice glances over at Diego. "Hurry up and take the damn picture, Theo," she says.

People generally do what Caprice tells them to. Theo is no exception. He shuffles a few people around. Then he snaps some photos. The moment he finishes, Caprice grabs her crutches and heads out.

At that moment, a movement behind the far bookshelf catches my eye. Someone has been flitting around there since Theo started arranging us for the photo. I know exactly who it is.

Fatima.

Chapter 21

Together

From where I'm sitting, I can see something that Fatima can't. Caprice is practically right beside her. When Fatima steps out from behind the bookshelf, she is face to face with Caprice. Fatima's mouth opens and closes a few times, but no words come out.

I hold my breath as Caprice pauses. I can't hear what she says, but Fatima slowly nods. Then she smiles a soft, wary smile.

The other kids from the Safe Grad

committee are drifting out the door. I turn to Mandy. "There's something I need to do," I say. "I'll text you later."

I shuffle over to the far bookshelf.

"Fatima?"

Her eyes dart between the floor and my face.

"I know you usually hang out here during the school year," I say. "But during the summer too?"

As always, her long, heavy hair covers most of her face. "I like it here," she says.

When she looks up at me, her hair falls back. My eyes land on the red, angry mark on the side of her forehead. Fatima recoils as though I just hit her. And I know instantly that someone did exactly that. Someone hit her.

The scared, haunted look in her eyes reminds me of myself. It reminds me of the time I lived under Duncan's roof and the months that Mom and I spent hiding from him. I'm getting the feeling that this isn't the first time something like this has happened to Fatima. Even Caprice beating her up in the hall wasn't the first time.

Shame flushes through me as I remember how I couldn't help Fatima in the hall that day. But now, maybe I can.

I'm trying to think of what to say when Fatima speaks up. "I read the news story about you and your mom." I have to lean in close to hear her soft, whispery voice. "I'm glad you're safe," she says. "You were really brave."

"Thanks." I take a deep breath. "I never thought I'd feel safe again. But if I can, then other people can too."

Fatima looks away, her eyes filling with tears.

"How about we go get a coffee or a hot chocolate," I say. "We could talk."

Fatima nods lightly. Tears keep dropping onto her chin.

"I think you're braver than you realize," I say. Then we leave the library together.

Acknowledgements

Although "thank you" feels inadequate, I wish to extend my heartfelt gratitude to these individuals:

My writer friends, who provide endless support and inspiration during our dog walks, lunches, and writing circles: Joan Marie Galat, Lorna Schultz Nicholson, Debby Waldman, Gail de Vos, Rita Feutl, Monique Polak, Caterina Edwards, Glen Huser, and Ann Sutherland.

My Indigenous colleagues and friends who shared their experiences and who encouraged me to write this book. Special thanks to Melody Callihoo for her friendship and her stories. Thanks also to Johanna and Vernon Wishart, author of *What Lies Behind the Picture?* and *Kisiskâciwan (Saskatchewan)*. Your generosity and encouragement mean a great deal to me. Like you, Vern, Vienna cherishes the *ceinture fléchée* that her grandmother gave her.

Jared Tkachuk, whose description of his varied roles as an outreach worker helped inform the work done by Jerome in *Saving Grad*. Although a fictional character, Jerome holds a special place in my heart.

I called on some experts to double-check my use of French — just in case! *Merci beaucoup*, Danielle Amerongen *et* Anna Fitz. I also called on Michael Spafford for technical support, and on Matt Spafford for advice about teen culture and phrases. Any errors, of course, are mine alone.

Thanks also to the Lorimer team for their confidence in both Vienna and in me. An extra special nod to my editor and friend, Kat Mototsune, who deserves armfuls of irises (deep blue ones, of course) for her kindness and her expertise in helping me shape *Saving Grad* into the story that it has become.

As always, I am eternally grateful to the three great loves of my life: Ken, whose belief in me never wavers, even when mine does;

Anna, whose devotion and convictions move mountains for me; and Shannon, who brings joy and laughter to all who meet her.
Thank you for sharing this journey with me.
I love you.